HERO

Also by SARAH LEAN

A Dog Called Homeless
A Hundred Horses

HERO

SARAH LEAN

WITHDRAWN

 KATHERINE TEGEN BOOKS
An Imprint of HarperCollins Publishers

Library of Congress Cataloging-in-Publication Data
Lean, Sarah.
Hero / Sarah Lean. — First U.S. edition.
pages   cm
"Originally published in the UK by HarperCollins Children's
Books UK."
Summary: An accident at school brings quiet, imaginative Leo
to the attention of the popular crowd but their expectations have
him misbehaving and cause him to lose his best friend, George, so
when a neighbor's dog is trapped by a meteor strike Leo becomes a
real hero in hopes of setting things right.
ISBN 978-0-06-212238-4 (hardcover)
[1. Conduct of life—Fiction.   2. Popularity—Fiction.   3. Best
friends—Fiction.   4. Friendship—Fiction.   5. Jack Russell terrier—
Fiction.   6. Dogs—Fiction.   7. Heroes—Fiction.   8. Meteors—
Fiction.]   I. Title.
PZ7.L46333Her 2014   2014005859
[Fic]—dc23   CIP
                                                              AC

Typography by Erin Fitzsimmons
15 16 17 18 19   CG/RRDH   10 9 8 7 6 5 4 3 2 1
❖
First U.S. edition, 2015
Originally published by HarperCollins in the U.K. in 2014

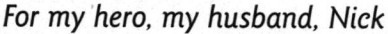

For my hero, my husband, Nick

One *

I can fit a whole Roman amphitheater in my imagination, and still have loads of room. It's big in there. Much bigger than you think. I can build a dream, a brilliant dream of anything, and be any hero I want. . . .

For the most awesome, heroic imagined gladiator battles ever, once again the school is proud to present the daydreaming trophy to . . . Leo Biggs!

That's also imaginary. You have to pass your trumpet exam to get a certificate (like my big sister, Kirsty), or be able to read really fast and remember tons of facts to get an A in school (like my best friend, George), before anyone tells you that they're proud of you. Your family doesn't even get you a new bike for your birthday for being a daydreamer, even if you really wanted one.

Daydreaming is the only thing I'm good at, and, right here on Clarendon Road, I am a gladiator. The best kind of hero there is.

"Don't you need your helmet?" George called.

"Oh yeah, I forgot," I said, cycling back on my old bike to collect it. "Now stand back so you're in the audience. Stamp your feet a bit and do the thumbs-up thing at the end when I win."

George sat on Mrs. Pardoe's wall, kicking against the bricks, reading his book on space.

"It says in here that meteors don't normally hit the earth," George said, "they break up in the atmosphere. So there aren't going to be any explosions or anything when it comes. Shame."

"Concentrate, George. You have to pretend you're in the amphitheater. They didn't have books in Roman times . . . did they?"

"Uh, I don't think so. They might have had meteors though. People think you can wish on meteors, but it's not scientific or anything."

He didn't close the book and I could tell he was

still concentrating on finding out more about the meteor that was on the news. So I put on my gladiator helmet (made out of cardboard, by me) and bowed to my imaginary audience. They rumbled and cheered.

"Jupiter's coming now. Salute, George, salute!"

The king of all the Roman gods, with arms of steel and his chest like hills, rolled into the night stars over Clarendon Road like a tsunami. Jupiter was huge and impressive. He sat at the back of the amphitheater on his own kind of platform and throne, draped his arm over the statue of his lion, and nodded. It was me he'd come to watch.

I held up my imaginary sword.

"George!"

George punched the sky without looking up from his book. He couldn't see or hear what I could: the whole crowd cheering my name from the thick black dark above.

Let the games begin! Jupiter boomed.

The gate opened.

"Here he comes, George!"

"Get him, Leo, get him good."

The gladiator of Rome came charging up the

slope. I twisted and turned on my bike, bumped down off the curb, and picked up speed. The crowd was on its feet already and I raised my sword. . . .

And then George's mom came round the corner.

"George! You're to come in now for your dinner," she said.

I took off my helmet and put it inside my coat.

"In a minute!" George said. "I'm busy."

"It's freezing out here," she said.

I skidded over on my bike. I whispered, "George! Please stay! It *is* my birthday. You have to be here, I have to win something today."

"I'm fine," he called to his mom. "I've got a hat."

"Yes, but you're not wearing it." She came over, pressed her hand to George's forehead. "You've got homework and you're definitely running a temperature."

"Gladiators don't have homework," I said. George grinned.

"But George does," his mom said.

"Mom!" His shoulders sagged.

She shook her head. "I think you both ought to be inside. Come on, George, home now."

"Sorry, gotta go." He sighed. He slipped off the

wall, pulled at the damp fabric from the frosty wall on the back of his pants. "I'll come and watch tomorrow."

"Do your coat up," George's mom said as they walked away.

George turned back. "Did you know that Jupiter is just about the closest it ever gets to Earth right now?"

I looked up. Jupiter was here, in the night sky over Clarendon Road.

"Yeah, I know, George."

"I'll do some research for our Roman presentation."

"Yeah, awesome, see you tomorrow."

"Leo!"

"What?"

He saluted.

I didn't want to go home yet though. I really wanted something to go right today.

I bumped the curb on my bike, cruised back into the arena.

The gladiator of Rome was lurking in the shadows between the parked cars. I could smell his sweaty fighting smell, hear his raspy breath. Just in time

I hoisted my sword over my head as he attacked. Steel clashed. I held his weight, heaved, turned, advanced, swung. We smashed our swords together again. I felt his strength and mine.

The crowd was up: thousands of creatures and men stamped their feet in the amphitheater of the sky. Their voices roared. Swords locked, I ducked, twisted, to spin his weapon from his hands. I didn't see the fallen metal trash can on the pavement. I braked, but my front wheel thumped into the side of it. I catapulted over the can and landed on the pavement.

The crowd groaned. Jupiter held out his arm, his fist clenched. He punched his thumb to the ground.

I'd never thought that I could lose in my own imagination. Maybe I wasn't even that good at imagining. I lay there, closed my eyes, sighed. It warmed the inside of my cardboard helmet but nothing else. Everything was going wrong today.

I opened my eyes, but it wasn't the gladiator of Rome looking down at me. It was a little white dog.

Two

I didn't know if dogs had imaginations or if they thought like us at all, but this little dog looked me right in the eye and turned his head to the side as if he were asking the same question that I was: How can you lose when you're the hero of your own story? Which was a bit strange seeing as nobody can see what's in your imagination.

I leaned up on my elbows and stared back. The dog had ginger fur over his ears and eyes, like his own kind of helmet hiding who he really was, and circles like gingersnaps on his white back.

"Did you see the size of that gladiator?" I said.

The little dog looked kind of interested, so I said, "Do you want to be a gladiator too?"

I think he would have said yes, but just then a great shadow loomed over us.

"Is that you dreaming again, Leo Biggs?" a voice growled.

It was old Grizzly Allen. He had one of those deep voices like it came from underground. If you try and talk as deep as him it hurts your throat.

Grizzly is our neighbor and the most loyal customer at my dad's café just around the corner on Great Western Road—Ben's Place. Grizzly was always in there. It was easier and a lot better than cooking for one, he said.

You might tell a dog what you're imagining, or your best friend, but you don't tell everyone, because it might make you sound stupid.

"I didn't see the trash can. I couldn't stop."

Grizzly held out his hand and pulled me up like I was a flea, or something that weighed nothing.

"No bones broken, eh?" He beamed. "Perhaps just something bruised."

I checked over my bike. The chain had come off and the rusted back brake cable was frayed.

"Aw, man!" I sighed.

"Bit small for you now," Grizzly said. "Can't be easy to ride."

"Yeah, I know. I need a new one." I shrugged, but I didn't really want to talk about that. I'd had this bike for four years, got it on my seventh birthday; the handlebars had worn in my grip. They were smooth now, like the tires and the brake pads and the seat. I didn't want to say anything about how I'd thought my parents were getting me a new one for my birthday, today. I guessed they didn't think I deserved it yet. It wasn't like I'd passed my Grade 6 trumpet exam, like Kirsty had.

Grizzly picked up my bike as if it were as light as a can opener, leaned it against his wall, and lowered himself down, all six feet four of him folded into a crouch.

"Can't do anything with this here cable." He sort of growled in his throat, but I didn't know if that was because he couldn't fix it or because he was uncomfortable hunkered down like that.

The little dog watched Grizzly's hairy hands feeding the chain back on the cogs. Grizzly didn't have a dog, and it looked odd, a great big man with that little white-and-ginger dog standing, all four legs square, by his side.

"Did you get a new dog, Grizzly?"

Actually there was nothing new about that dog, except he was new here on our road. I don't mean he looked old, because he didn't. He was almost buzzing with life. There was something ancient about him though. Like one of the gold Roman coins in our museum. Sort of shiny and fresh on the outside, but with years and years of history worn into them.

"He's not mine," Grizzly said. "This here is Jack Pepper." The little dog watched Grizzly's broad face, and his tail swayed at the sound of his own name.

"He belongs to Lucy, my daughter. She's asked me to look after him for a couple of weeks while she takes herself off for some vacation sunshine over the other side of the world." He winked at Jack. "We're keeping each other company for a bit."

Grizzly steadied himself against the wall, so I offered him my shoulder to help him up. He was heavy. His joints creaked and clunked like a worn-out machine and he groaned. Jack Pepper stood between us, looking up as if he wanted to know everything that was going on with Grizzly so he could help. Jack didn't seem to understand that he wasn't even as tall as my knee.

My bike was twisted, but Grizzly held the front wheel between his knees and pulled the handlebars with one almighty yank until it was straight again.

"Should do it for now," he said, "but you'll have to get down to TrailBlaze to see if they can do something about those brakes."

He looked at me for a long time before nodding toward the fallen bin and the trash strewn along the pavement. There was a smell of rot and something sharp.

"Jack had his nose to the front door, so we came out to look and see if cats were getting in the rubbish."

"I didn't see any cats," I said. "Mrs. Pardoe's big orange cat went in Dad's shop once and stole a chicken sandwich, right off the side."

"And who wouldn't want some of your dad's delicious food, eh?" Grizzly laughed. "Hear that, Jack? Maybe I'll be treating you too!"

I picked up the bin, then the empty soup cans and old tea bags, and threw them back in. Jack Pepper sniffed and sniffed. He didn't seem to mind whether they were good or bad smells; he just enjoyed sniffing them. I tried to put the lid back on, but it was bent and didn't fit properly.

Grizzly took the bin and put it back in his front yard, rested the dented lid on top.

"Best keep this out of your way, hey son?" He smiled, his small eyes shining under his broad lined forehead. He nodded toward my helmet. "Hard to see out of that, eh?"

"Oh, this!" I took my cardboard gladiator helmet off, embarrassed that I'd forgotten I had it on. But Grizzly wasn't laughing at me. He seemed quite impressed actually. "It's for a presentation on Romans we have to do at school next week. I'm a gladiator, but I don't like standing up in front of the class."

"Why's that then, son?"

In all the imaginary battles that I'd fought on Clarendon Road I could make things turn out just how I wanted (except for today). But things weren't like that in the real world.

I shrugged. "The kids at school always look bored whenever I talk about something, and our teacher doesn't notice you unless you're really clever or really stupid. They think I'm lame, and that gladiators are too. But they're not."

"I see." Grizzly frowned. "George helping you with your presentation?"

"Yeah," I sighed, "he's better at research and words than me. I made this instead." I held out my helmet to show him. "It's made of cardboard, but I painted it."

Grizzly beamed. "Would you look at that!" he said, peering closer. "Thought it was real bronze for a minute."

"Yeah?"

"Had me fooled!"

I liked that he said that, but then I checked the helmet over and saw that the crest had been crushed when I fell.

"Maybe I should redesign it or make some more armor, you know, like for protection or something."

"So it matters what other people think, eh?" Grizzly said.

Of course it did.

Grizzly called Jack Pepper to come in, closed the

gate, and headed for his front door. The little dog stopped and stared at me through the bars of the gate.

"Tell your dad I'll see him Friday," Grizzly said. He whistled for Jack Pepper to come inside, but that little dog stood there for the longest time with his tail quivering as if he'd rather come with me and be a gladiator too. Grizzly whistled again and Jack followed this time, still watching me, and I thought I heard Grizzly say, "He won't win battles by having better armor, will he, Jack?"

Three

Everybody had heard about the meteor that was coming our way. They said we'd even be able to see it flash across the sky from here. I looked out of my bedroom window and imagined Jupiter frowning down at me, disappointed that I'd lost my latest battle.

Jupiter was king of the sky and thunder; he held lightning in his bare hands, ready to hurl it at anybody who annoyed him. I wondered if he threw meteors too. I imagined Jupiter resting his chin on his fist.

Where's the show then? he grumbled. *Where are all the gladiators?*

My little sister, Milly, came into my bedroom and stood beside me by the window. She pressed her head against the pane and looked up at the empty sky.

"Is the meteor coming?" she said.

"No, not yet," I said.

Mrs. Pardoe's ginger cat was in the road though and I watched it to see if it was going to Grizzly's trash can.

"What are you looking at then?" Milly said.

I picked her up and sat her on the windowsill. "Look. Watch its shadow."

The cat trotted through the beams of the streetlights.

"It's a small cat . . . now it's growing and growing . . . now it's huge!" The shadow shrunk and grew, shrunk and grew again, as the animal trotted along the pavement. "It's pretending to be a lion."

"Is it?" she gasped.

The cat slunk along, pressed tight against the wall, its tail swinging and twitching.

"It's stalking, catching prey," I whispered, making it all dramatic.

Milly's eyes were wide. "You mean it's chasing

a mouse, but actually it's pretending it's going to catch a . . . a hippopotamus?"

I don't know why she said hippopotamus. "Well, yeah, but probably an antelope or zebra, that kind of thing."

"It's like real but not real," she said, "and magical." I smiled. The cat disappeared over a wall. Milly sighed. "Will you come downstairs now? We're all waiting."

"Hang on a minute," I said. I thought I'd show her the helmet and see what she thought, see if she could imagine it too. "Close your eyes a second."

"I can't close my eyes," she said, dead serious.

"Why not?"

"When I do, I keep seeing the meteor and it scares me. What's going to happen to us?"

"Nothing's going to happen," I said. "It's just going to burn bright for a minute and then it'll be gone. It'll be pretty. You'll like it."

"Really?" Then she leaned over and whispered, "Tell me the truth. Do you love your new sneakers the best?"

I looked down at my feet, turned out my ankles.

"I helped pick them," she said, staring at my feet

too. Milly was only six. I couldn't tell her that I was disappointed I didn't get a new bike.

"They are the absolute best sneakers ever," I told her. I put on my Roman helmet, with fierce eye-holes and a terrifying square mouth and curved crest on the top, now held up with sticky tape. "Tell me the truth. Do I look like a gladiator?"

"No, because I know it's you." Milly giggled. "Now come on, we've got a treat."

"Cool sneakers, hey, son?" Dad said from the sofa, taking up two spaces as usual. He spread his hands out toward the coffee table. "We've got all your favorites, plus . . . secret ingredient on the chicken." He winked and chuckled.

"Garlic," Mom said, with a knowing nod, and went out to the kitchen.

"Chocolate?" Milly said. "Could it be chocolate?"

"Chili," Kirsty said. "I think it's chili."

We did this every time, tried to guess what that extra-special flavor was. We'd probably guessed right a long time ago, but Dad would never tell.

"What do you think, Leo, my little dreamer? What's your best birthday guess?"

I shrugged. "I don't know."

"Leo doesn't know much about anything, apart from playing gladiators!" Kirsty said. "Don't you think it's a bit babyish playing pretend games? No wonder you've only got one dorky friend."

Kirsty had loads of friends and everyone liked her, but they didn't know how mean she could be sometimes.

"I think it's lovely," Mom said, before Kirsty and me could argue (although gladiators were not lovely!). She was coming back from the kitchen with my birthday cake. It was all lit up and ready to blow out. "Here we are. Dad made it specially."

Three sponge layers oozed chocolate cream with a load of candies all spilled over the top. Awesome.

"As it's your birthday, you can have cake first," Mom said.

"Can I as well?" Kirsty said. "I am the oldest."

"And me," Milly said.

"We'll all have a big piece of cake first." Dad grinned.

"Are you going to make a wish?" Milly said.

I blew out the candles, thinking it was a long time until next year to get a new bike.

Four

"Stop it, Leo," George said, spinning around on his computer chair. "You're supposed to be helping with our presentation."

"I'm doing research," I said.

"Yeah, right." George swung back to his computer. "Write your ideas down. And get off my bed, you're messing it up."

Sometimes I'd forget what I was supposed to be doing and be battling a new gladiator, swept away by the roaring crowd. If I wasn't doing that on Clarendon Road I'd be at George's house and he would help us do our homework (he did most of it). George liked books and words. They were his favorite things.

"George?"

"What?"

"How come things from the past are so deep under the earth? I mean, where did all the stuff on top of ancient ruins come from?"

The Romans left a ragged flint wall here, in our town, straight as an arrow along the back of the recreation field, which you can still see. They left pots and coins and buckles and pins in the earth, which we stared at when Mr. Patterson, our teacher, took us on a field trip to the museum. We stared at the artifacts and I imagined all the people who might have owned them, wondering about what they were like and what their stories were. Were some of them gladiators like me?

"I don't know," George said. "It's erosion or compost or something."

I opened his book on Romans to find something interesting. I looked at the pictures and caption boxes and read one out.

"Romans invented amphitheaters and arches, and realistic-looking statues, socks—"

"Socks?!"

"That's what it says, socks and baths, and a law

that we still have today, which says you're innocent until proven guilty."

"Although if you're guilty you know you're guilty, even if nobody proves it," George said.

"There was also a man called . . ." I passed the book to George because it was one of those words that looked impossible to say.

"Ptolemy," he pronounced. "Toll-a-me. It's a silent *P*."

"Oh, right. Anyway, he mapped the stars and joined the dots and named them after a whole mysterious collection of mythical beasts and animals and gods and heroes. I think I would have liked him, George."

I had posters of the universe and everything in it stuck up in my bedroom. You could get posters inside Dad's newspaper every Sunday for free until they covered your ceiling.

I put my gladiator helmet on and saluted to the sky out of the window, to the audience of the stars. I thumped my arm to my chest.

"I will return," I said, and punched my imaginary sword in the air, just to hear the men and gods and monsters cheer.

"Leo!" George said. "The helmet's good, but do I have to do everything else myself?"

"All right, grumpy," I said.

I fell back on his bed and crossed out my three lines of notes and tried to write them again. Something weird happens between your imagination and your pencil. I tried hard, really I did, to describe what it was like to be a gladiator. It all felt real and bold and brilliant inside my helmet— and when I was on Clarendon Road with a cosmic crowd to cheer me on—but it was dull and lifeless on paper.

"George, I think I need your help or I might end up letting us down."

"Give it to me," he said.

He typed out some of the information from his book. George had enough words for the both of us. He printed out a few pages and handed me two sheets. Lines and lines of words and paragraphs.

"You can read that out in class," he said. "It's lots of facts about gladiators."

"Do you think we should have some pictures in our presentation?" I asked.

He sniffed. "I'm not doing any more. I don't feel

well and I've got a headache. Anyway, it'll be good."

I wasn't so sure. This presentation was like a battle all on its own, and I needed backup, even for George's excellent words. I fell on his bed, let the papers float to the ground. I needed to do something so that Dad, Mom, Mr. Patterson, and the kids at school would know I had a good imagination, that I was good at something, not just relying on George.

"What if I acted out a gladiator battle? Maybe with a tiger or something?"

George did his you-are-kidding face. George is good at knowing when you need to be invisible. "In front of the whole class?" he said. "In front of Warren Miller?"

It was a warning, not a question, and we both knew I wouldn't do it.

Kirsty said there's a Warren Miller in every year at school. Ours was the new boy. He walked into our class in September with his chin in the air like he was looking way ahead of us. Some people just have it, whatever "it" is. Everyone tried to impress him, until he gave them a soft punch in the arm and sealed their popularity fate. Or not.

Warren ignored me and George. Everybody

usually ignored me and George. Except Beatrix Jones, but then she's kind of unusual. George and me sat together in class at the far-side desk of the middle row. It's like a blind spot, which is good for not answering too many questions, but bad if you do want to get noticed. For something. Just once maybe.

"Anyway, we won't need any of that," George said. "You've got your helmet and I've made this."

From under his desk he pulled out a cut-out-and-build-your-own amphitheater, made from white card stock.

"Nobody else will have anything like this. What do you think?"

George has a different sort of imagination from me. I didn't say what I was thinking, that perhaps he should have colored it in before he built it, or drawn people in it.

"Impressive," I said, because he isn't usually good at arty things, and because he's my best friend. But I had a horrible feeling that nobody was going to be impressed by either of us.

Not in the real world.

Five

eorge was out sick from school.

I was daydreaming out of the window, reliving the battle with the gladiator of Rome and making it turn out differently, with me winning. Then I was thinking about Jack Pepper and that he didn't know how small he was, when Mr. Patterson called my name.

"George isn't here," I said, which I thought was a good enough excuse to get me out of doing the presentation.

"You can do your part," Mr. Patterson said.

But I'd left the papers at George's house, and, for some stupid reason, all I could remember about our presentation was the gladiator's battle with the tiger, which I'd already sensibly decided I wasn't going to do in front of our class. Especially Warren Miller.

So there I was in front of everyone, wearing my helmet, trying to explain about gladiators, but I wasn't good with words like George.

"There's sand on the floor, like a beach, but obviously it's not a beach, and there's trapdoors. So then the tiger comes out. . . ." I wasn't sure how to show that, so I snarled instead, "Grrrr," and swung my coat. "This is a net and . . ." But I couldn't be the tiger and the gladiator, so I said, "Mr. Patterson, will you pretend to be the tiger?"

Mr. Patterson nodded and kind of hunched his shoulders and made his hands like claws, frowning like Warren Miller was.

"And this is supposed to be a sword . . . or it can be a trident, which is like a garden fork. . . ." I had Mr. Patterson's yardstick and chopped it in the air a few times. I thought about describing the different types of gladiators, but it was easier just to make slashing noises and let the class imagine what I was.

Then, just when I was getting even more anxious

about how to end the presentation, I swept the stick around low but hadn't seen that Mr. Patterson was going to pounce and accidentally tripped him. He fell, sprawling across his desk, knocking books, pens, and papers all over the floor.

Everyone burst out laughing and Warren Miller started chanting, "Le-o! Le-o! Le-o!" Then all his friends joined in. My cheeks burned and I couldn't say sorry to Mr. Patterson because my throat was dry and squashed shut, but he just smiled and said, "That was a very enthusiastic presentation, Leo. Perhaps we've learned that gladiator helmets may have restricted their view somewhat." He told the class to be quiet.

I'd really let George down, but I was hoping I could rescue things.

"George made an amphitheater," I blurted out. I wanted Mr. Patterson to know that we'd done some good things for the presentation, I just didn't have them.

"I'd like to see that," Mr. Patterson said. "You can sit down now, Leo."

He crawled behind his desk to pick up everything and I ducked my head and went back toward the empty space where George should have been. How was I going to tell him later that I'd really messed up?

"Nice one, Leo," Warren said from the back of the class. He grinned, showing his sharp crooked tooth. "Who'd have thought, you of all people."

"I didn't mean to do it," I said.

"Even better." Warren laughed.

I was rigid, humiliated and waiting for more sarcasm.

"Come and sit with us," he said. Laughter rippled through the back row. "No, I mean it. Move up, Josh. Come on, Leo. We could do with someone like you. I like your style."

He beckoned me over.

I couldn't believe what was happening. Not only was it totally unexpected, it was pretty awesome too. I didn't know what to say or do so I sat next to Warren, and he put his arm across the back of my chair. Warren's big. Not big and lumpy like Josh, but as if he's somehow more than a boy. More than me anyway.

He leaned across and whispered, "See what I can do for you?"

I think what he meant was that he was like one of those Roman senators who had a say in what happened to you. Thumbs-down: nobody cares. Thumbs-up: you're in. So just like that, Warren Miller made me a kind of hero, even if it was only in front of our class.

"We'll resume presentations next week," Mr. Patterson said, standing up again.

"I hate presentations," I whispered to Warren, and that got me a soft punch in my shoulder.

I was pumped. It was like riding high in a golden chariot after beating the gladiator of Rome, and it felt like the whole universe of Roman gods and Jupiter were on my side too, because Mr. Patterson said, "I think we'll call it a day. You can all go home five minutes early."

Warren nudged me and was out of his chair.

"Our next project is about space," Mr. Patterson called after the swarming class. "You've all heard about the meteor passing over the town in a few days. Perhaps finding some photographs from the internet and doing some investigation into what's up there in this universe of ours would be a good place to start."

The room clattered with knocked chairs and pushed desks as we rushed past Mr. Patterson to leave.

"Perhaps you could avoid reenactments of colliding planets or big bangs when we do our space presentation, Leo," Mr. Patterson said.

"Sorry about tripping you," I said.

It was easy to say now, but I didn't exactly feel sorry for the effect it had.

Warren was waiting for me at the bike shed on his bike: all shiny black paint, twenty-one gears, and orange reflectors on the spokes. Josh and the swarm gathered around him, chanting, "Le-o! Le-o! Le-o!" again. Waiting for me. Warren flashed his crooked tooth with a half grin.

I grinned back.

He said, "Meet us at the recreation field tonight at seven. We could do with a gladiator on our side."

Six

It wasn't just people that gladiators had to fight in the amphitheater. Sometimes there were beasts. These were the ultimate kinds of battles for a gladiator. The thing about battling animals was that they were unpredictable. You couldn't count on them behaving like men or other gladiators at all. You had to have your wits about you, and after what had happened at school, I thought I was ready.

When I went out to Clarendon Road after school for another epic battle, I didn't take my gladiator helmet because I was going to the recreation field straight after. I wasn't sure whether Warren really meant that he wanted an actual gladiator on his side. Maybe he just meant someone like me, brave or something like that. Anyway, I wore my bike helmet instead, because it was easy to pretend it was a gladiator helmet.

I rode into the arena.

Jupiter was on his feet; like a tower block in a toga he loomed in the sky at the end of Clarendon Road.

It's time! he boomed to the audience. They were climbing down the amphitheater steps, rushing to the edge of the arena to get a better look. After what happened at school I felt like a gladiator on a whole other level. I nodded, held my hands up.

"Okay, okay!" I said. "You all need to stay back. I don't want people getting hurt." It all felt so easy.

Send in the bear! Jupiter roared.

The audience caught their breath as the bear padded through the open gate and into the arena. I smelled the sharp smell of him; he huffed, snorted, growled. He lumbered in and showed me his broad head and his rugged side, rippling with thick hair. He was huge, but I wasn't scared because I knew I was quicker than him.

I swerved around him on my bike, going close, pulling away as he swiped his massive paws. I turned, raised my sword, checked the crowd. On their feet now, they roared my name and I knew I could have defeated that bear with them cheering me on . . . except Grizzly Allen came out of his house and leaned over his wall. And you don't want someone else watching, unless it's George of course.

Grizzly was bundled up in his coat and scarf and cap against the cold winter evening. He beckoned me over. I used my heels to slow down. Jack Pepper peeped through the bars of the gate; his tail swished and I crouched down to say hello.

"Off to see George?" Grizzly said. "I heard he's not well."

Grizzly was often outside by his wall, talking to anyone who passed, which is why he probably knew what was going on most of the time. Jack Pepper panted as if he'd already been running along the street beside me.

"No, just playing around."

"Don't want to catch anything, eh?" Grizzly winked. He folded his arms, which were too thick to fit easily together. "You've heard about the meteor passing over?" he said. "A fragment of our far universe come to shine on us. A little magic to light us up, perhaps to bring us a bit of good fortune, eh?"

I think he said that because all the adults were gloomy around here. Even Dad sometimes. Business hadn't been so good, like at all the other shops in town. More had closed than opened and they even knocked one crumbling building down.

"Mom says winter makes people sad," I said.

"So it does," Grizzly murmured. "Feels like time and the light forget us for a while."

He looked up. "All that space up there," he said. "Look at it all. Miles and miles above us, a never-ending place, full of possibilities." He smiled at the depth of the sky. "When you look up there, do you feel like there's more than what our eyes can see, hey, son?"

"Yeah," I said, because I did.

"Good," he said. "Now do an old man a favor and take Jack Pepper out with you, there's a good lad. My legs won't manage it today."

Jack Pepper had that look about him again, like he knew what I was thinking.

"What time is it?" I said. Grizzly pulled back his

sleeve and showed me his watch, as big as Dad's alarm clock. I still had some time before seven.

"Okay, come on, Jack," I said.

Grizzly opened his gate. That little white dog came right over and stood next to my bike, looking up, like he was ready and he knew what we had to do. Grizzly turned and shuffled back toward the open front door.

"Door'll be unlocked, so just drop him off when you're done." He leaned on the porch and looked back over his stiff shoulder. "Take good care of him," he said, but I wasn't entirely sure that he was talking to me. "And don't be going down to the recreation field just now."

I didn't know why he said that. I guessed it was to do with Jack Pepper being used to walking around the block and not in the open fields.

There's something about dogs that isn't like people at all. The way they're kind of ready and willing. Straightaway I knew Jack Pepper didn't think that pretending to be a gladiator was a waste of time.

"There's a bear, Jack," I whispered. "He's here somewhere, waiting to ambush us."

I pushed up on my pedals, felt my bike as if it

was part of me, twisting and turning and speeding up, Jack running alongside.

"You're gonna have to be quick and not go too near. Just do what I say, stick close, and you'll be fine."

Jack Pepper joined in, leaping beside me, ears twitching as if he was listening out for the bear. We were like a couple of soldiers, advancing in formation, and I didn't have to ask him, he just moved like my shadow.

We approached the bear, growling, huffing, and breathing his hot, bitter breath into the frosty evening.

"That way, Jack!" I said. We separated. Jack distracted the bear, dancing around him, barking and yipping until we'd cornered him outside Mrs. Pardoe's house and roared at the beast until he lay down and rolled over for us.

Jack sat beside me in the glow of the streetlight and gazed up like he could see what I could see.

The winners! Jupiter bellowed and punched his mighty thumb to the sky. All arms went up; everyone cheered my name. *Le-o! Le-o! Le-o!*

"Bow, Jack, bow!" I said. "They love us." Jack

wagged his tail. "Look at us," I said, grinning down at him. "We're heroes."

When I looked up again, Jupiter had reached down and touched the head of the statue of the lion by his throne. I saw the lion shake the dust from its fur. I saw it open its mouth, come to life, and roar.

I took Jack back to Grizzly's and opened the door for him. He went in but stopped and looked over his shoulder at me, like he didn't want to go home just yet. I heard him whine when I closed the door, but there was somewhere else I had to be.

Warren and all his friends waited in the shadow of the ragged flint and moss of the ancient Roman wall along the edge of the Rec. Warren walked out from among them, slow and easy. There was a lot of whispering, which for some reason sounded louder in the dark, with only the moon and stars and a couple of streetlights making yellowy circles around us.

"Wasn't sure you'd come," Warren said. He sighed. "Thing is, some of us still aren't sure you've got what it takes to hang out with us. You're going to have to prove yourself first."

"I thought I already had," I said.

"You have to do something else . . . to prove you're one of us," he said. The boys parted, showed what they had for me. "You have to push it down the field and send it into the pond."

I looked at the old granny mobility scooter that they'd found, and it bothered me.

"Whose is it?" I said.

"It was abandoned out the back of the pharmacy," Warren said. "We took it, hid it, and waited till dark, waited for someone like you."

"Why do I have to do it?" I said.

"We have to be sure you're on our side," Warren said.

"It doesn't work then? It's not somebody's?"

"It's useless. We're doing everyone a favor by getting rid of it, cleaning up the town." There was a ripple of laughter, but Warren silenced the others. He paced up and down. "Fame," he said. "They say it's a fifteen-minute thing." He draped his arm over my shoulders. His armpit was a bit rank. "But you want more than that, don't you, Leo? You're proving that you've got what it takes to be one of us."

I wasn't going to be a gladiator in the real world,

not when the nearest we have are boxers and wrestlers. I wanted to be like a gladiator though. I wanted other people to think I was fierce, brave, strong, and worthwhile. Which was entirely different.

I dropped my bike. Took an uneasy breath. Walked over to the scooter. They couldn't see what I could see: me, the victor, and the abandoned chariot of a defeated gladiator.

"Le-o!" they chanted again.

The moon made a shimmering target on the dark pond, like a trapdoor in the amphitheater where all the destruction, the losers, the broken and defeated things go. I pushed hard against the mobility scooter and ran with it, down the slope, and let it go. The scooter tipped over into the pond. It bubbled and sank, disappeared into the black depths. I punched the air. They laughed, roared, and cheered my name. It made my teeth tingle. This was being a gladiator for real.

Seven

School for the next few days was completely different. Fist-bumping all over the place, back-patting, sitting in the back row, being one of Warren's friends while George was still out of school. I was famous now. People I hardly even knew were asking me to take out their teacher!

I was following Warren and his friends to our corner (our corner!) of the playing field at break time when Beatrix Jones caught my sleeve. She stood in front of me, narrowed her eyes, and asked, "Why's George not here?"

"He's sick," I said.

"Hmm." She scowled. "Sick of what?"

I shrugged. I didn't know what she meant.

"I'm surprised," she said.

I hesitated. "He's got the flu. Why's that surprising?"

"Not about George, about you."

I guessed it was a compliment, that she was surprised I'd done something people noticed and was now one of the popular kids.

"Thanks," I said.

She huffed. "I mean surprised you've been fooled by Miller, idiot!"

Beatrix Jones was weird, so I didn't listen.

I went to catch up with Warren, which was when I overheard him saying to Josh to spread the word that they were meeting at the recreation field again on Friday after school. The message didn't exactly get given to me, but I didn't have anywhere else I wanted to be. The thing is, once you've tasted fame, you just can't get enough of it. You know when you've eaten half a bag of chips and you're saving the rest for later, but you go back to the kitchen to finish them after only a few minutes of waiting, plus you get a piece of cold chicken from the fridge and maybe some cheese? That's what fame feels like. A feast.

So, on Friday, I went.

Warren was leading the others across the field, all of them on glossy newish bikes. Warren looked down at my bike, at the torn seat, the clunking gears, the tires worn smooth. Then I didn't know what to say. I wasn't exactly invited this time. My bike was half the size of his and everyone else's, and the brakes had just about had it. "Hey," I said. "What are you all doing?"

Warren grinned.

"We've got business in town. Private business. Maybe see you some other time."

"Yeah, sure, I was just, you know . . ." But he wasn't listening.

Warren's knees bent, he yanked up the front of his bike, and they cycled past while I cringed inside. My cheeks flamed. I kept my back turned. Why had things changed so quickly?

Behind me I heard barking. It was Jack Pepper, darting around in front of Warren's bike. What was he doing here? Warren twisted and put his foot down quick, but Jack ran away. He tore past me, turned, and raced back, straight toward me. He stopped, looked up. I didn't know what he was doing there or asking me to do.

Warren called my name. In the second it took to look at Warren, Jack Pepper whipped past me again. Warren skidded over, rippling up the turf, and stopped beside me.

"Changed my mind," he said. "Help us catch the dog."

I hesitated.

"You're with us, aren't you?" he said, but it didn't sound like a question. "Leo! Get the dog. Do it for us."

So I had to decide.

I was just going to get Jack. That's all. I thought he would stop for me. I had to prove myself again. Anyway, what was the worst that could happen?

Warren zipped past me, gaining on Jack Pepper. He circled round and herded him toward the rest of his friends coming back across the field. I saw an opportunity. Up on my pedals, I pushed hard and headed toward the pond. I saw all the others on their bikes closing a circle, corralling the dog toward me. I was almost at the edge of the pond and whistled. Jack tore across the field, straight toward me, then he turned sharply in front of me. I braked. The wheels didn't stop. The back of the bike skidded across the damp grass, slipped from under me.

I couldn't put my feet down.

There was nothing underneath me.

I fell into the pond, pulling my bike on top of me.

Cold water thumped the air out of my lungs. My legs kicked against something sharp under the water. It was all I could do to swim up and get the bike off me.

"Help me out!" I panted.

Josh and the others dropped their bikes and for a moment I thought they were coming to help. Jack raced back toward me. One word from Warren and they rushed at the dog from all sides. I was left there with the cold biting my skin, my jaw tight, my teeth aching, trying to hold on to the grass at the edge.

Jack barked, like a much bigger dog, protecting a small territory in front of me.

"No, Jack!" I breathed.

Warren looked down at me, twisting his hips to try to balance the bike. I put my head down to try to lever myself up, but my breath was all gone.

Then I heard the yelp. The surprise cry of pain

from the dog when Warren and his bike toppled and landed on Jack Pepper. The sound from Jack got in my teeth and my eyes. It tested something inside of me. I tried to shout, but the bitter cold had taken my breath and my strength, and I could only wheeze, "You shouldn't have done that!"

"It was an accident!" Warren said. Then, just like that, he changed.

I saw everything evaporate, all the power drain from me, in that one moment. Warren growled, a sound like dissatisfaction in his throat.

"Let's go," he told the others.

I heard the click of chains on their bikes as they all left. Someone said, "Leo's gone to get the mobility scooter back," and they laughed.

I grabbed some reeds, heaved my chest up, waited, and breathed. And then I felt that little dog's teeth on my wrist. I flinched, cried out. Jack softened his mouth and tightened his jaw around my coat sleeve. I felt that tiny dog pulling.

Eight

I sat there, dripping. I trembled and shivered, too cold to move or breathe. I couldn't believe they'd left me there, that Warren had hurt Jack. I couldn't shake that away, even if it was an accident.

Jack was holding a back leg up off the ground, but his face wasn't saying anything about that. His ears were folded, up bright, like he was saying so many things except anything about the hurt.

He watched me intently, looking at my leg. My pants were ripped. I'd gotten blood on my shin too. I wiped at it, but it kept trickling and dripping. Jack hopped over when I put out my hand and it was like an extra punch in the stomach, because I thought he was asking if I was all right even though his cut looked a lot worse than mine.

I looked around, but there was no one there. I was glad that nobody else had seen that I had been part of this. But I just wanted Jack to go. That would have been easier because then I wouldn't have to admit I was involved in what just happened. But he didn't budge. I thought he was waiting for me and it was a long way home without my bike.

I closed my eyes and tried to wish him away. But that didn't work either.

Jack Pepper hopped beside me. He stopped to lick his leg. I thought he must be expecting something from me. I was shivering so much and I couldn't feel my hands, but I hooked that dog under my arm and headed back.

Grizzly Allen's door was locked. I knocked. I called through the mail slot, but there was no answer. Jack Pepper licked his leg again and I knew I wasn't going to tell Grizzly what had really happened.

I couldn't think. I was so cold I just wanted to lie down and sleep.

I headed on down Clarendon Road, the dog in my arms, him looking up at me like he was still waiting for something from me. Still checking I was all right. But, because of him, I'd probably lost everything I thought I had. There was no way Warren would ask me to hang out with him again. Right then I just wanted to get rid of that dog and the way he looked into me, like he knew what I'd sent to the bottom of that pond and wondered why.

My head was weird and dreamy when I heard them murmuring and whispering. The audience in the amphitheater muttered and shuffled, but I didn't know what they were saying.

"You're not supposed to be watching this," I said. "There's nothing to see. This isn't one of the battles."

I looked up at the empty space where Jupiter usually loomed over the crowd and when I looked back there was something in the road that shouldn't have been there. Jupiter's lion walked along the white lines in the middle of Clarendon Road.

He turned when he saw us, padded onto the pavement toward me and Jack Pepper, all casual, like we were going to meet. He looked like he owned the pavement, like this was his hunting ground, the houses were his hills and the streetlights were his trees, and I was in his way.

I stopped. Jack Pepper wriggled under my arm and I didn't know if I had the strength to dodge the lion. I didn't think I should put Jack down, even though he wanted me to. I hunched him closer.

The lion slowed to a walk and sat down. It began to rain, but the lion just sat there, only a few yards away, looking like a fire in the hearth. His golden eyes and wide nose glistened as if he was inspecting us through our smell. I was tired and weak. *It's just my imagination. It's not real.*

I headed out to the road, skirted round the parked cars. I saw the lion between the cars, head low, watching as I passed. Jack Pepper whined, twisted in my arms; his legs paddled in the air as if he wanted to go after the lion.

We were nearly at my house when something made me look back through the pouring rain. Mrs. Pardoe's ginger cat was sitting on the pavement just where we'd stopped, as if he was claiming our space for himself.

Nine

D ad sat on the toilet lid, a hand under my armpit to stop me from slipping under the bubbles in the bath. I couldn't talk, my teeth chattered too much. My head felt strange and nightmarey.

"It's the shock, but you're all right," Dad said.

I wasn't all right though.

The towel was warm. My bed was warm. But my bones were still cold.

Jack Pepper was next to me. I felt the warmth of him against my back. He was looking over my shoulder, and just the way he did that was too much. I closed my eyes because right then he was like some kind of beacon, lighting up, showing everyone the things I wished I hadn't done or been involved with, the things that I wished hadn't happened.

"Where did the dog come from, son?" Dad asked.

I imagined myself in the arena, the gladiator of Rome about to charge again. A great shadow fell over me. I was about to lose everything.

"I rescued him from the pond," I lied.

Ten

D ad cooked breakfast. He was by the stove with a tea towel flipped over his shoulder, cracking eggs with one hand like the real pro he was. He had opera music on the radio and boomed out a song. I'd even been allowed to wear pajamas at the table.

Dad made up his own words to the ice-cream song: "Just one more sausage and fried potat-o! Delicious breakfast for my Le-oooo!"

He handed me a plate with a Dad-sized heap of food.

"A man's start to the day!" He winked. He kept

singing, ruffling Jack Pepper's fur, scooping him up and kissing him.

"And my boy saaaaved the dog, this gorgeous doggy, Jack Peppereeeeee-y!"

He swirled the tea towel over his head, kissed Jack one more time, and threw another slice of bacon in the frying pan.

"So you jumped in the pond to save the dog," Kirsty said. "And the dog got hurt on a shopping cart someone had dumped in there?"

She was repeating the story I'd told them. I nodded. It was easier to lie about what happened with a mouthful of toast, while Dad puffed up with pride and chucked my chin.

Milly fed pieces of sausage to Jack Pepper, who was under the table, i.'s swishing tail tickling my leg.

"Air's best for his leg to heal," Mom said. "I phoned Grizzly last night and told him the dog was here. He said he wasn't worried because Jack was in safe hands." She ruffled my hair, which felt uncomfortable, and I patted it back down. "Jack escaped through the gate when Grizzly went out of the front door to pick up his garbage can. Cats keep knocking it over, he said. He couldn't manage walking the streets to look for him and thought Jack would come home by himself. You're to take him back when you're ready, Leo."

Mom went to leave for work but then stopped.

"Who were you out with yesterday?" she said.

I put a big piece of sausage in my mouth and started chewing so I couldn't talk. I shook my head.

"No trouble with anyone else then?"

I swallowed the lump and it stuck in my throat.

"Just me," I choked. But it was unnerving that she seemed to know to ask questions like that.

"Thought so," she said. "Your dad and I did wonder. It's not like you to go down to the Rec."

She left for work, saying everybody home by five for supper, we've got visitors coming. All I had to do was eat that mountain of food and then take the dog back.

"So your bike's still at the Rec, right?" Kirsty said.

I looked at Dad, but he wasn't listening: he had bacon to turn. It wasn't going to make sense to say the bike was in the pond. Why would the bike be in the pond if I'd dived in to save the dog?

"Yep," I said, "I couldn't carry both back."

Dad glanced over. "Grizzly said he bumped into some trouble down at the recreation field recently."

Did Grizzly mean Warren Miller? I didn't want to know.

"Tell me again why the dog was in the pond?" Kirsty pressed.

"Fell in," I said, concentrating on balancing as many beans as possible on my fork.

"Leo dived in after him, no thought for himself. What-a-boy!" Dad said. My head was down, shoveling egg.

"Good thing you weren't lost in one of your gladiator daydreams, or you probably wouldn't have even noticed," Kirsty said.

Dad told Kirsty to stop teasing, that I'd had a bit of an ordeal.

"Leo's a hero," Dad said. "We should all be proud of him for rescuing Jack Pepper. Wait till I tell my customers!"

I imagined it—Dad telling everyone about me—and that was the thing about being a hero, people wanted to spread the news.

"Aw, Dad. You don't have to tell everyone. I mean, it was nothing."

"Don't have to tell everyone! You think I'd want to keep something like this to myself?"

Then Dad bear-hugged me. He was proud as anything, he said. I grinned. Finally, I'd done something great. Me!

Jack Pepper yipped and wagged and jumped and tried to get on my lap. Kirsty rolled her eyes, but I could see the corners of her mouth turning up. She was enjoying the moment too. It was good. Even though it wasn't true.

Dad smiled. It was like the sun beamed out of him even through the gray gloom of winter.

"I'll have a chat with Mom later," he said. "Money's very tight, but we'll have a think about a new bike for you as a reward for being so brave." He winked.

And then it was easy to bury the things that I didn't want to think about. Like a dog's forgotten bone.

Eleven

Jack Pepper wriggled to greet Grizzly when I took him home.

Grizzly checked him over. Jack's leg seemed better already and he was hopping only every other step and too full of something else brighter to care about his injury.

"Causing mischief, were you, my boy? Trouble and worry, running out the door," Grizzly said, even though there was nothing going on but delight at having that dog back. "Lucky Leo found you, eh, Jack?"

Jack Pepper didn't care what had happened. I wasn't going to say anything about Warren and his friends, what they did. And I guessed they wouldn't dare either. Nobody needed to know and nobody would get in trouble.

"Want to walk Jack again today?" Grizzly said. His eyes twinkled under his cap. "He's really taken a shine to you, son."

Jack was waiting by my feet as if he'd already decided we were going out together again. Maybe there were new battles he wanted to fight with me, but taking him out now wasn't really going to be a good idea. I kind of needed to get away from him for a bit. Besides, what would I say if I bumped into Warren? And what would he do? It was going to be easier to avoid him and his friends.

"No, you're all right, Grizzly," I said.

"Sorry, Jack," he said. "I expect Leo's off to see George. He won't want a mischief-maker hanging around, what with him being a hero and all that."

I'd lied, but I hadn't lost that feeling that people were proud of me.

"Another time," I said, and was about to go. Only for some reason I didn't feel like going to see George either.

"I was a bit of a hero in my day too," Grizzly

suddenly said. "You know why they call me Grizzly?"

I didn't, although I guessed it had something to do with the fact that he was the size of a great bear.

"Because you're big and hairy?" I said.

He laughed, like a pirate. "Used to be a boxer, many years ago."

Grizzly stepped one leg back and rested his weight on bent knees. Joints popped and clicked as he stumbled, growled, and steadied himself. His fists closed, elbows high, big powerful arms protecting his head. He punched the air, showed me his moves.

"In 1968, I took out Nicky Sullivan. Boof! Just like that. Didn't see me coming."

An old match played in his memory. He commentated, ducked, and cuffed the air. I got in there in the dream and the ring with him, with Nicky Sullivan, the champion boxer.

"Go on, Grizzly!" I cheered under the spotlights and between the ropes. I laughed because I thought that maybe Grizzly might know what it was like when I was on Clarendon Road with my gladiator helmet on while he sparred with his imaginary gloves. He talked of punches and blows and moves, defense and attack, his feet shuffling when they should have been bouncing, his shoulders jarring when they should have been flexing.

"You have to keep your guard up," he told me, "to protect your head. You need your body fed and fit for fighting, your heart strong for winning, but your head clear for thinking. If you don't protect your head you can't think straight, can't predict the move you need to make."

Grizzly towered; his fists recalled a fateful jab. Jack Pepper leaped and barked at the ghost of Nicky Sullivan and Grizzly's triumph.

Grizzly's hip clicked and the fight was soon over. Jack licked his leg again.

"After that fight they called me 'The Bear,'" Grizzly said.

"Did you knock him out? Was he out for the count?"

Grizzly counted him down, dancing unsteadily around as if Nicky Sullivan lay at his feet.

Grizzly roared with laughter. "Saw stars, he did, oh yes."

He lowered his arms, turned kind of thoughtful.

"It was my daughter, Lucy, who called me Grizzly, Grizzly Bear, years later when she was a little girl and I told her about Nicky Sullivan. Said that fight made me her hero."

I thought that must have been good, having a boxer for a dad, but the way he said it, slowly, softly, and almost like he regretted it, made me think Lucy knew something else about Grizzly that we didn't. I know dogs can't speak, but I swear Jack Pepper was listening to every word Grizzly said.

"Just take Jack round the block," Grizzly said, quick as a punch, smiling at Jack, snapping out of his dream. "He won't mind."

I figured I owed him that much. I looked down at Jack. I saw in his bright eyes that he wanted to come with me.

"Keep your head down," Grizzly called from the door. "That meteor's coming over soon."

Twelve

Jack Pepper didn't need a leash. He was there beside me, one eye on my legs.

It was different this time. I thought about how easy it had been to make my family proud, and I hadn't even really done anything. But I liked it; I liked feeling like another person. And it was all because of Jack. I owed that dog a lot.

At first the ground wasn't moving fast enough underneath me. My legs were twitchy and I felt heavy without my bike. The memory of the bump of the curb was still there, the handlebars that fitted in my hands. Then I started running, twisting, turning, stopping, backing up, like I could have done on my bike, and that dog just fell in with me. I could dart sideways or run or slow down and he'd stick right there with me.

I felt good, like I had a lot of victories under my belt. I thought up a good battle for me and Jack.

"I'll be the gladiator," I told him. "You . . . you can be a lion this time."

Jack Pepper squared himself up, tilted his head to one side.

"We're not going to fight each other though. You're my lion and I've raised you from a cub. We'll do this battle together."

Jack's tail swished and I knew he had my back: we were a pair of gladiators together, a team. The way a dog looks up at you like that, you just know they're going to stick by you and fight to the end. It was easy to forget what really happened with him at the pond because Jack made me feel like his hero anyway.

Jack Pepper followed me to the end of Clarendon Road. We turned left.

"The bear's come back, Jack! Watch out! Over the other side, look, Jack! The tiger! You can get him, Jack, go on, you can get him!"

We took them on both at once, circling and dodging. We defeated them with swords and teeth, had them lying obediently at our feet. We were on a roll and there was more to come. Jack Pepper was a mini gladiator, fierce and fearless in a much bigger way than he looked. I didn't miss my bike, not one bit.

Send in the gladiator of old! Jupiter roared. We took him on with his net and trident, and Jack leaped and barked until we knocked him down and he saw stars, and I put my foot on his chest and punched the air to the roar of the crowd.

Jupiter spread his arms and clenched his fists and thumped his thumbs to the sky. The charioteer galloped into the arena and circled us, holding wreaths of laurel leaves. He bowed down and put them on our heads to an almighty cheer.

"We did it! We're invincible, Jack!"

Filled with our triumph, we set off to North Road, where the shops were. We were still buzzing, but there was a kind of dull hum hanging about our town.

Nothing ever happened here. The council built the bike park last year, but then everyone complained because not many people used it and what a waste of money, and it didn't even bring more people into the town. So they started a market, which was open today, and we joined the slow march of people bundled up against the cold while we were warm and fizzing.

Jack's just about the friendliest dog ever, because loads of people stopped and talked to him. Actually he stopped and talked to them. Not talked exactly, but, you know, like he had something to say. He'd look at them in that kind of bright way and, if he could have talked, he'd probably have told them about the battles we'd just won.

People checked their shopping bags for a biscuit or a treat.

"What's his name?" they asked. "Is he yours?"

And I said, "He's called Jack Pepper. He's Grizzly Allen's dog—he's looking after him for his daughter."

"Oh, didn't someone say something about a little dog like this and a boy who rescued him from the pond?"

I imagined Dad in the café, and Grizzly hanging

over his wall, stopping anyone who passed to tell them the tale. The story bubbled through the market.

"You're Ben's boy, aren't you, little Leo Biggs?"

Everyone knew my dad; everyone liked him as soon as they met him. Some of us have to pretend to rescue a dog from a pond first.

My face flushed. I grinned. It wasn't just my family and Grizzly who knew. Everyone did! I started to walk like Jack Pepper. My feet bounced off the pavement because it felt good walking with that little white dog in his ginger mask. I couldn't help it: I just let them tell me what a hero I was. It was the best feeling in the world. Being noticed for something like this. Being famous for saving a dog.

"I remember you from a few years ago," the fruit and veggie man said. "Always down Clarendon Road on your bike."

I had history now: they remembered things about me, linked me to their past, felt so glad they knew me. It seemed like it made them better, made them happy, just by knowing me and Jack.

Jack was interested in everybody and he spread

a smile from one person to another. It was magical, the way he'd nudge someone's leg, wag his tail, and they'd light up at him and our story.

I filled in details about what had happened, things that made the story of rescuing Jack Pepper even bigger.

"He was terrified and I just had to help him," I said.

"So what was it that scared Jack Pepper?" someone asked.

"Uh, maybe a cat. I saw Mrs. Pardoe's cat earlier, you know, that big ginger one? There was a fight; the cat chased Jack and he was so scared he jumped in the pond."

"And you jumped in after him?"

"Yep, sure did."

"Marvelous."

"What a hero."

"What a brave thing to do."

"Could have been dangerous," someone gloomy said.

"Nah," I said, brushing away the doubt. "I knew I could do it."

Soon I had this extra story changing bit by bit to

suit anyone who asked. I basked in the glow of all the praise.

"Lost my bike though. Had to leave it there and it's probably been stolen by now," I said, feeling the sympathy brewing around me.

"No! What a shame."

"I'll have to go without one for a while. Dad says things are a bit tight, but anyway, he's going to have a think about a new one, you know, maybe." It was hard to look disappointed, but I did my best.

The lady from the pet-food stall gave Jack a raw-hide bone to chew.

"Hey, Bill! Sheila!" she called to the other stall-holders. "Perhaps we could have a fund-raiser; poor lad's lost his bike and his family can't afford a new one."

I went up to the window of TrailBlaze and looked at the bike that I wished for. I stood so my reflection and Jack's were right by that shiny new bike.

"See that?" I said to Jack. "Suits me, don't you think? And I reckon it won't be long before it's mine."

Everything was different now. Once you've tasted fame, like dad's chocolate cake with chocolate sauce, you'll make room for some more even when you're full. Which is why, on the way back home, Jack and I took on two more gladiators at once. And Jupiter kneeled before us.

*Thirteen *

I didn't want to take my gladiator lion back to Grizzly just yet. Holding on to Jack Pepper, having him with me, made the whole feeling of being a hero more real.

Our five o'clock visitors were at our house when I got home with Jack. George and his mom. I hadn't exactly been avoiding George, but I hadn't thought about him much.

"Do you want Coke or Fanta, Leo?" Kirsty said when I came in the back door to the kitchen. "No, wait, there's no Fanta left. George had the last bit."

"Coke then," I said.

I watched George through the crack of the

kitchen door, perched tidily on the sofa in his tidy clothes with his tidy hair. He had a book on his lap. I didn't know why, but suddenly he didn't seem to fit in very well with how things were now.

"Unless you want two straws to share with George?" Kirsty laughed, but I rolled my eyes.

"Is Jack Pepper allowed Coke?" Milly said, even though she'd already poured some in a saucer on the floor.

"I don't think he should—" I said, but Milly wasn't listening.

"Oh, it's okay, he likes it," she said.

"Leo, is that you?" Mom called. "Come on in. George is here."

The whole family was home and they'd brought the kitchen chairs into the living room because there wasn't enough room for everyone to sit down otherwise, what with Dad taking up two seats on the sofa. Dad patted the small space beside him for Jack Pepper. He jumped up there, licked Dad's face, and then climbed up and curled over his belly.

There was excellent food from the café for everyone, of course, and napkins and paper plates to save on washing up. In between laughing at Jack because he had hiccups, we were discussing the meteor.

"It'll burn and break up when it reaches our atmosphere," George said. "By the time it reaches the ground it'll just be tiny fragments."

He held up his book on space and looked as if he was about to say a whole load more about the meteor, so I said, "We get it. It's going to burn bright and we're all going to like it."

George frowned. I shrugged. I could do nothing wrong.

"Will it be like a wishing star?" Milly said. "You know, like when we find the brightest star and wish for something?"

"Definitely," I said. "All your dreams will come true."

"Will they?" Milly said. "Dad, will they?"

"Nicely said, son," Dad said. "Something to wish on." Then he toasted me with a can of beer.

While they all shared wishes, George leaned across and said, "Where've you been?"

Just a few days without him and suddenly he looked like a different person to me.

"School. Home," I said.

"Your dad told us about the dog, what you did."

For some weird reason, it was harder to talk to George about it than anyone else. I just kind of nodded a bit. Then he whispered, "I've got a question though. I thought dogs could swim?"

Typical George! Why hadn't I thought of that? Why hadn't anyone else? How long would it be before somebody did? Why hadn't anybody else noticed the big hole in my story?

Then George's mom said, "He's a nice little dog. Good thing Leo's helping to walk him." She smiled at Jack Pepper, who was stretched out, legs dangling around the curve of Dad's middle. "Such a shame about poor old Grizzly."

"Isn't it?" Mom said. "He should have had that hip replacement when they offered it to him."

"You know Grizzly though," Dad said. "He's been on about getting a mobility scooter, but the man's too proud to be seen in town on one."

I didn't know if I was imagining it or not because I obviously couldn't see if my face was as pale as it felt when all the blood drained out. It was like two comets were hurtling across the universe on a collision course, and it was inevitable what would happen when they met. I felt it coming: bad, bad news.

"People have been wondering where Grizzly's been, not seen him in town just lately," George's mom said. "Turns out he did buy a mobility scooter and somebody stole it."

BOOM! The comets collided. The scooter I'd pushed into the pond belonged to Grizzly. But I hadn't known!

"When people lose their cats, they make posters and stick them up on lampposts," George said. "Leo, shall we make a poster for Grizzly's scooter, just in case someone's seen it?"

"Did Grizzly lose his cat?" Milly said. "I didn't know he had one. Mrs. Pardoe's got one. Is her cat lost?"

You know that horrible feeling when you wish you could go back and change things? It's called guilt.

George screwed up his eyes and stared at me.

Milly said, "What color is the cat?"

Everyone was trying to explain to Milly. It felt like the whole audience of the amphitheater was there, all talking at once, all booing, hissing, turning down their thumbs. I couldn't hear myself think.

"Have you been back to look for your bike, Leo?" Kirsty suddenly said.

"Did you lose your bike?" George said.

I wanted them to stop asking questions.

"He left it at the pond when he rescued Jack Pepper."

Jack Pepper sat up and looked at me. I wasn't sure if it was because someone had mentioned his name or because he was interested to know what I'd say. I swear that dog knew what everyone was talking about.

"What's wrong, Leo?" Kirsty eventually said. "You've gone really pale."

George grabbed my arm, as if he knew I was ready to run, to escape what seemed like a trap closing around me.

I shook off his arm and headed for the stairs. George and Jack jumped up and followed me.

I stared out of my bedroom window, breathing fast, shocked by what I'd heard, not sure what to do. Warren had lied about the abandoned scooter and I had lied about rescuing Jack Pepper from the pond. We were both as bad as each other.

Jack was on my bed, his paws on the windowsill, watching, whistling softly through his nose.

George was silent. And that made it worse. I stopped myself from telling George even though I was on the verge of spilling my guts. I sat down on my bed, buried my head in my arms. George wouldn't understand. I mean, even in my own head it didn't sound like something I'd do or something that he'd like about me.

"Shame you didn't get a new bike for your birthday like you thought you would," George said. "But then it would have been your new one you lost, so probably just as well."

"Yeah, yeah," I said. For some reason, George talking about it kind of made it irritating to hear about again. I felt angry. I wanted him of all people not to be here right now. He looked around the walls and at the constellations on the ceiling like he'd never been in my bedroom before and it was all new and interesting.

"Something else happened, didn't it?" George said.

"No, it didn't!" I snapped. "It's none of your business anyway."

"Just tell me," George said.

"No," I said. "I'm going out."

Fourteen

I ran. Jack Pepper ran with me. I hated the fact that he was sticking by me when . . . when it was his owner's dad that I'd done this to. Why didn't Jack understand? I wished he did. I couldn't bear to have him looking up at me like I was still his hero.

I turned onto Great Western Road, let the buzz and roar of the traffic drown out the shame in my head. It was Grizzly Allen's mobility scooter. He needed a hip replacement. He couldn't walk well. How was I supposed to have known? If anyone knew the truth about what had happened, they'd think that I was trying to hurt Grizzly on purpose.

I ran along the pavement until I reached the empty lot where an old shop had been knocked down. I climbed through the chicken-wire fence that somebody had cut and peeled back so people could dump their trash in there. I sat down in the middle of the garbage, and I hated that Jack came and sat next to me.

"Why do you have to be so loyal?" I shouted. "Why don't you just leave me alone? I wish I'd never met you!"

Jack's tail swished once and his ears dropped.

"I didn't mean for this to happen." I groaned.

Questions spun around inside my head. How long would it take for people to forget that I was the "hero" who had rescued a little dog from the pond? Would I ever live down ruining Grizzly's scooter if everyone found out the truth?

Just then George turned up. He had followed me too. He curled his fingers in the wire, staring at me from outside the fence. I didn't know what was stopping him from questioning me more. He knew something was wrong.

Eventually George said, "Beatrix Jones dyed her hair pink." He fiddled with a bit of loose wire and my stomach surged. "I think it's kind of cool," he said. "Changing yourself like that."

George crawled through the hole in the fence.

"I saw her in town earlier."

"And?" I said. It was like being in a dark alley, not knowing what was going to leap out and get me. I couldn't stand it if George knew about the scooter or about me not really saving Jack Pepper.

"I prefer Beatrix out of everyone else in our class, except you, Leo."

I shrugged. Still waiting, not really hearing anything except for the pounding of blood in my ears.

"But I don't understand why you are trying to be friends with Miller."

I felt like a gladiator on his knees in the sand without a shield, waiting for a stronger gladiator to deliver a killer blow, but in the end George said, "I suppose some dogs aren't that good at swimming."

George let me off the hook and I didn't deserve it, but it just made me more angry. Mad that he was a much better person than me.

"Don't you have homework or something?" I said.

He stood there for ages not saying anything, and

then I couldn't believe it: Warren and his friends cycled up to the fence.

"What are you doing?" Warren said, kind of half friendly, half smiling with his crooked mouth, through the crooked wire. I couldn't speak. It felt like there were too many gladiators in the arena. Warren probably thought I'd told George about what happened with Jack Pepper.

I looked at George.

"Nothing," I said, because I needed him to know that I hadn't told George. But it came out all wrong. It sounded like I was saying George was nothing.

Warren's eyes held mine, but he spoke to George.

"Did you hear that Leo saved this dog from the pond?"

I swallowed, hard. Jack Pepper's legs were stiff and quivering. The wiry hair on his back stood up and he growled, but he looked at me as if he wanted a word, a sign that he should do something about Warren Miller and his friends.

"I know." George hesitated and I worried that Warren might think that meant more than it actually did. "So?"

"You're a hero, aren't you, Leo?" Warren smirked because I think he could tell that George didn't know any more than that. The bike twisted under Warren as he tried to keep his balance. "Come on, Leo. You belong with us. We're going down to the Rec. We've got something else for you."

I glared. Jack growled like a much bigger dog. I had to keep on Warren's good side though. I couldn't risk him saying anything about what happened with the scooter and the dog, not to George, not to anyone.

Surely he wouldn't, not without letting on that he'd stolen the scooter and hurt Jack Pepper. We were bound together in this. We had to trust each other, which felt all wrong, because if one of us fell, one of us said anything, then we were both going to go down together. But I didn't want any more challenges. Not from Warren Miller.

I saw a question in the twitch of Jack's eyebrows when I hooked my fingers under his collar and pulled him toward me.

"I've got to take Jack back to his owner. Stupid dog ran off again." I didn't mean it. I just hoped

Jack Pepper didn't understand what I was saying.

"You're all right, Leo," Warren said. "You're still one of us. See you later then." It felt like a threat, not an invitation.

Before I'd even gotten up, Warren cycled off, looking back with that half smile that really bit me, like he'd gotten me all worked out now.

George huffed, folded his arms like it was the first time he'd ever done it and it was a complicated thing for him to do. He narrowed his eyes.

"What?" I said.

"Oh, nothing," he mimicked. I felt the sting in my cheeks and the tightness in my throat. "You've changed, Leo," he said. "All of a sudden you think you're it just because you hang around with them. Maybe you're the one that's nothing."

"At least I don't dye my hair to make me more popular!" I snapped.

George flinched liked he'd been stung by a wasp.

"At least Beatrix and me don't pretend to be something we're not."

That hurt more than anything else because it was true.

"It's Beatrix and me now, is it?"

"Yes," he said, without hesitating. Then he said, "I'm going. I don't know what I'm even doing here with you."

Then George was the one who left. He didn't look back. He left me there. Part of me wanted to shout out to George and tell him the truth, but I couldn't find the strength to do it.

Jack Pepper saw the cat before I did, before I had the chance to think any more about what had just happened. The dog leaped out of my arms as Mrs. Pardoe's ginger cat slunk past the back fence. Jack whined, his tail flicked, his ears were high and trembling. He ran up and down looking for a way through. The cat kept his yellow eyes on Jack, but there wasn't a twitch of fear in his fur.

Why wasn't the cat scared of Jack? I thought dogs chased cats. Something twisted in my stomach. I'd told people the cat chased Jack! Somebody was going to question my story sooner or later. But why had the cat slowed to take a good look at Jack?

I couldn't move fast enough when I realized that Jack was looking toward the hole in the wire at the front of the lot! I threw myself at him and tackled him down to the ground, then scooped him up in my arms. He was startled. He licked my face, but twisted round to look over my shoulder. The shadow of a big, big cat, with a shaggy ruff around its neck and wide padded paws, twitched its tail and disappeared around the corner.

I took the dog back to Grizzly's, found the door unlocked, and put Jack inside, telling him, "Don't you ever be a hero, Jack Pepper. It's not worth it."

Fifteen

Ge**orge** wasn't at school again. Warren and his friends were quiet behind me in class and I didn't dare look at them. I hid in the bathroom at break.

It felt like this was going to be the longest day ever, as if time had slowed, like it was just as disappointed as me at the way things turned out. I didn't want to be famous anymore.

I didn't feel like fighting any gladiators on the long walk home after school. I could imagine the crowd groaning.

Where have all the heroes gone? they shouted.

"There's nothing to see," I said. "Not today."

We want a show, we want a battle!

They threw rotten tomatoes and hard crusts of bread at me; they hissed and booed. I kept my head down, ducking unwanted food and disapproval, disappointment that I had nothing worthwhile for them.

Grizzly Allen was leaning on his wall, bundled up against the cold with a thick scarf. It was too late to cross the road to avoid him. I couldn't not speak to him, but I dreaded him mentioning his scooter.

"The meteor's coming today," Grizzly said as I passed him. I couldn't look him in the eye.

"Everyone's going to wish on it. How about you, Leo?" he asked.

I ignored the question and crouched down. Jack blinked slowly while I scratched his head through the bars of the gate.

"What do you think a dog wishes for, Grizzly?"

"Not much," Grizzly said. "Probably a good bone to chew or a tickle of his belly." There was warmth in his answer, like these were probably the finest wishes anyone could make. As much warmth as

Jack had in his eyes right then. All bright and just happy that I was telling him to sit, then lie down or give me a paw.

"A dog doesn't ask for much, except for loyalty. And he'll give it back in return," Grizzly said.

Grizzly's bin was tipped over again. He growled as he picked it up, collecting the chicken bones, empty tomato-soup cans, and cookie boxes scattered in his front yard.

"Is it that cat getting in the trash again, Jack?" he muttered. "Not trash to the cat though, is it? It's a rich feast to him." He laughed. "He doesn't know what he's doing is wrong."

I scratched the ginger marks on Jack's back.

"He's a good dog, Grizzly," I said.

"Is he now? Running off out of the gate that time?" He was smiling with all that sunshine inside him again. "Lucy didn't get him to be a good dog. No, no." I didn't understand. "She says Jack makes her feel brave. There's goodness about him all right, but not the ordinary kind."

Grizzly got it too. That Jack Pepper wasn't asking anything much from us.

"You'll be wanting to take Jack Pepper out again then, Leo?"

I nodded. There was something I had to do, and for some reason I thought it would be a lot easier if Jack Pepper was with me.

Sixteen

Jack was at my heels again. He made our walk, every step, important, all the way to the corner of Great Western.

The dummies in the dress-shop window were wearing winter fur coats. George's mom worked here and I knew he'd be inside, probably reading a book. I walked past the shop a few times, thinking about what I was going to say.

George had been my friend for a long time. It couldn't be right that we didn't fit together anymore. This fame thing would all go away soon. Then I'd be the same old Leo again. George hadn't done anything wrong. He had never made me do anything that I shouldn't, not like Warren.

I stuffed my hands in my pockets and stared at the dummies and my own reflection in the window. I couldn't leave things as they were.

I told Jack Pepper to wait outside, knowing he would. He sat, watched every step I made, and I wondered then what he was thinking. Even though I thought he could see through me and the bad things that I'd done, he didn't care. It didn't matter to him what I'd done; something else was far more important. That helped a lot, and that's how I could go in and face George.

The door pinged when I opened it. Jack waited, leaning forward to watch me through the glass. There were no customers in the shop, only George's mom coming up the stairs from the cellar with a box of hats.

"Hello, Leo," she said, and I guessed by the way she was pleased to see me that George hadn't said anything about us falling out.

"It's like a zoo in here," I said, because of the fur coats everywhere.

"Lions and tigers and bears." She smiled. "Oh my!" Then she leaned over and whispered, "Glad you're here. See if you can cheer George up. He's not been quite himself recently. Maybe that nasty flu took it out of him."

She put a golden fur hat on my head and laughed.

"Suits you," she said, but I pulled it off and it made my hair staticky and when I tried to pat it down it just got worse.

I slowly made my way over to squat on the windowsill next to where George was sitting, reading a book.

He stared at my hair.

"Positive electrons," he said. "It's because there's no humidity in the air. Wet your hand."

I licked my hand and pushed my hair off my face. It sort of worked. I touched the sleeve of the deep orangey fur coat on the dummy in the window.

"Fake fur," George said without looking up. He twisted his body away from me. "They're all fake."

I pushed back the hairs with my thumb; they were pale underneath.

"It looks real to me."

George huffed. This was all too heavy and difficult and I didn't know what else to say without it sounding like I was talking about us.

"Come out for a bit," I said.

George shook his head.

"Please," I said, but he ignored me, so I fiddled with a coat sleeve. George waited for ages before he pointed to a spotted black page in his book that looked like the connect-the-dots constellations on my bedroom ceiling.

"I'm busy with something important," he said. "I'm reading about Sirius."

"What's serious?"

"Sirius." He sighed. "Sirius is the brightest star in the night sky. It's also known as the Dog Star because it's part of the constellation Canis Major."

I looked at a diagram box, at the description.

"The eye of the Great Dog," I read.

I glanced through the window, at Jack Pepper with his nose against the glass, watching.

"Look, can we just forget what happened, George?"

"What has happened?"

"Nothing." I'd said it again, nothing, and this time I saw why that word made George's shoulders go tense and his breathing get loud. It wasn't because George thought I was talking about him. It was because I hadn't told him the things that were something. That's what best friends are for. That's why Jack Pepper stood by me and I hadn't even said sorry to him. Friends just want to know what's going on with you.

But I couldn't tell George the rest. Things had gone too far and I wasn't sure if he'd accept it all, not now.

"I just want to go back to how things were," I said. I even wanted to take back being a hero.

Suddenly there was a commotion outside the shop. A car horn blasted. Engines revved, more car horns. I looked through the window, saw people gathered on the pavement, their mouths wide open. Jack was still waiting, his ears cocked, his eyes turned to the sky like everyone else.

I pushed up against the glass. The intersection was at a standstill. All the cars had stopped at the traffic lights and everybody was leaning out of their windows. I don't think they saw what I saw. Jupiter throwing something across the sky. A huge glowing ball left an arc of smoke and fire, like a cut through the sky. Unzipping it.

"The meteor!" I said.

George dropped his book and pressed his face to the glass.

And then . . . BOOM!

A sound punched into my chest. People outside crouched, covered their ears. The earth shook from the explosion; windows shattered. We ducked as if it would reach us. Glass tinkled as it spilled across the road. When I looked up again, the slash of fire in the sky had curved over the buildings away from us.

Then there was a soft sound of relief from everyone outside. Applause. I looked at George. His mom had come over, and she had her hands up to her face and her mouth was open and her eyes were shining.

"What was that noise?" she gasped.

"Sonic boom!" George breathed. "That's what it was. A shock wave. Truly spectacular."

I couldn't stop looking at the sky. At the dust sprinkling down from the roof of a building across the way. My skin prickled. Something else was happening.

And then there was a rumble.

I couldn't tell where it was coming from.

It was far away and close at the same time.

I didn't know what was happening. The ground felt like jelly.

KABOOM!

Another thundering explosion.

Through the window I saw the whole middle of the intersection crack and crumble.

The ground collapsed.

Dropped.

Fell away.

There were deep thundering, breaking, ripping sounds. Car horns were on full alert. Car alarms, shop alarms, fire alarms all going off at once, hammering in our ears. People in the street ran. I looked up and saw a crack rip like lightning across the join of the window and the ceiling.

"Run!" George's mom yelled, grabbing us both.

We pushed fake fur coats out of the way to get to the door.

"Keep running!" George's mom shouted, flinging the door open. "The shop's coming down!"

We ran. Everyone was scrabbling to get away from the intersection. Dust and car alarms clogged the air; with the aching sound of bending metal, overhead wires sizzled, snapped; glass smashed.

Groaning and screaming, gagging dust. We kept running.

I turned to look back. The whole front of the shop tipped forward. Bricks, roof tiles, the door, the window, all the dummies buckled and collapsed into the cavernous hole.

My eyes stung from the thick dust that was blooming, growing, rising, gagging my throat. I rubbed my eyes and blinked and looked at where the intersection of Great Western and North Road used to be.

There was nothing but a massive hole there.

Seventeen

There was an empty space about thirty yards wide in the middle of our town. The intersection had gone. Caved in. Disappeared. The air was full of dust and sirens.

George's mom held on to me and George.

"It's a sinkhole!" George gasped. "The sonic boom must have shaken something underground."

"Sinkhole?" I repeated, watching firemen helping people out of their cars, telling them to come away, backing everyone up the street.

"A sonic boom creates vibrations. Sound can do that, break things."

More sirens grew louder. Fire engines, police,

ambulances, coming from all directions toward the intersection. But not too close.

"The ground must have been unstable already," George said. "Maybe burst pipes had eroded the ground underneath."

George talked and talked about rocks and erosion and stuff and then I couldn't hear him because I was replaying the last few minutes over in my head.

"There probably wasn't anything holding up the surface anymore," George said.

The hairs spiked on my neck.

I couldn't blink. My mouth was dry.

There was nothing but a hole where Jack Pepper had been sitting.

I got on my knees. Jack Pepper wasn't under the parked cars.

There was dust on everyone. People looked like ghosts; they shook and cried, breathed hard, their mouths open, but I pushed them aside.

I ran in circles; my eyes darted to every small space where Jack might be hiding, calling for him through the din of sirens because I couldn't bear to think what I was thinking.

"Did you see him, George?" I yelled. "Did you see Jack Pepper when we came out? Did you see him, George?"

I called, I shouted, "Jack Pepper! Jack!" I tugged at people, asking, "Did you see him, did you see a little white dog?"

No. No. No.

"George!" I shouted. "Help me look! Help me look!"

He shook his head. His eyes were full of panic.

"Jack Pepper's not here," he said.

My eyes stung. My chest caved in like a bottomless sinkhole. I looked up at the sky, at the meteor's vapor trail left across it, collapsing and falling down. I'd left Jack Pepper on the pavement. I'd told him to wait.

Eighteen

I was sinking.

Falling.

There was nothing I could say about the fact that it was me who left Jack Pepper on the pavement outside the shop that collapsed in the sinkhole. Me who told him to wait. Me. Why did Jack Pepper have to be such a good dog?

Dad's belly was soft. I didn't deserve to be there, with Dad holding me, kissing my head, wrapping his arms round me.

"You're still a hero in my eyes," Dad murmured. "You rescued Jack Pepper from the pond. Nobody can take that away from you, son."

The girls huddled together on the other sofa. Milly held tight to Kirsty. Kirsty's silent tears nearly killed me.

"It's not your fault, Leo," Kirsty said. "If anyone could have saved him it would be you."

I didn't know how to get back from here. I didn't know how to tell the truth about everything now. The weight of people thinking the wrong thing—even if they thought I'd done something good—pressed down on me. I didn't want to be that boy anymore. The fake hero.

It was three hours since the sinkhole opened up on the intersection, since a dark hole opened up inside me.

"What's going on down there now?" Dad asked when Mom came in.

Mom's sigh devastated me.

"The fire department is still checking if the ground and surrounding buildings are safe. They're keeping everyone away."

"What about . . . did anyone . . . ?" Dad asked.

"Nobody's missing, just a few bumps and bruises. Seems everyone was away from the intersection, distracted by the meteor. Lucky when you think about it." But I saw then how much she wished she hadn't said that.

"What are we going to do?" I said.

"We go back there and tell them there's a dog missing," Kirsty said.

"We need to let Grizzly know," Dad said.

Thump. There was a chasm the size of a black hole inside me and it was swallowing me up.

"Look, we can't be sure that's what happened," Mom said, crouching down, touching each one of us in turn. "What if Jack Pepper ran off? For all we know he could be sitting outside Grizzly's front door right now, waiting for someone to let him in, or he's already inside in the warmth with not a scratch on him."

"Someone's going to have to go and find out," Kirsty said.

My heart pounded in my ears. Once you did something that made your family proud, their expectation of what you can achieve next is even higher.

It had to be me.

I sat on a garden wall three doors down from Grizzly's house. I was bracing myself because I had nothing on the inside holding me together right then. And I didn't know what I was going to do if Jack Pepper wasn't there.

I walked up to Grizzly's gate. I spent a long time in the tiny front yard and porch, checking behind the bin again and again, checking every tiny space as if he'd shrunk and might even be under a pebble.

Jack Pepper wasn't waiting outside.

I knocked, stared at the door, and waited.

The hall light came on. Grizzly's shadow appeared behind the glass that was like weird frost, making him look shattered.

He opened the door. I looked past him into the hall to see if Jack was at his heels. If he would come and greet me.

"You're all right, aren't you?" Grizzly said. "What a terrible thing I heard today." And he looked past me too, to see if I had anyone at my heels. "Nobody hurt?"

I swallowed. "Did Jack Pepper come home?"

There was just Grizzly breathing because I don't think I could. I thought I heard his heart creaking, like the ache of rusty hinges on a closing castle door.

"Leo?" he asked. It was only my name, one small word, but I felt all the hope and pride in me evaporate like Grizzly's heavy breath in the cold night in his porch. Disintegrated like the tiny remnants of the exploded meteor that fell and scattered into the sea off the coast. Grizzly's eyes looked far away. I wondered if he was thinking of Lucy.

"I'm sorry," I said. It didn't sound like my voice; it was as if it came from the bottom of a pit. But I meant it more than anything else.

Grizzly rested his hand firm and warm on my shoulder.

"You've nothing to be sorry for," Grizzly said. "I could have asked anyone else to walk him, but I wanted you to do it. He wanted to go with you."

"He's a clever dog though, Grizzly, isn't he? He might have run and hidden somewhere," I said. "I'll find him."

I saw Grizzly's chest heave, and I think if his legs could have managed he'd have run out of the door and up the road right that moment to look for Jack with me. He steadied himself against the doorframe.

"I'll keep looking," I said. "I'll call and shout and keep looking."

"That's it, son. I know you'll do your best."

"I'll keep trying," I said.

I turned left at the other end of Clarendon Road. I called, I shouted into the night, I kept looking. I turned left again onto North Road, but I couldn't go any farther because the road was blocked off with police and emergency services guarding people against our broken town.

I turned back, retraced my steps. I looked in all the places I looked before, under cars, behind walls, next to bins, in doorways, and all the places I thought I'd missed. I knocked on someone's door.

"Have you seen a little white-and-ginger dog? Have you seen Grizzly Allen's dog?"

"No," they said. "Is it that little dog we heard about? Do you know the boy who saved him from the pond? Ask him—he might know."

I slid down the wall and hunched on the pavement in the shadow between the lampposts. In my mind I tried to blame Mrs. Pardoe's cat, for knocking over the trash, for making me fall off my bike, for meeting Jack Pepper, for everything. It made me angry; it made me mad as anything.

The lion stood on the white line in the middle of Clarendon Road. Like he was waiting for me.

I got up and walked right up close to him. He couldn't do anything to me; he was just in my imagination.

"I'm not moving for you!" I yelled at him. "You don't belong here! Jack does!"

He didn't move for me either. He turned his broad nose to the air and his eyes to the sky. His ragged mane fell back; his mouth opened and he grumbled a breathy growl. I saw the abandoned amphitheater up there. Jupiter had gone. Everyone had gone. Nobody wanted to watch me anymore. There was a star though, brighter than all the rest, holding its place in the sky. Sirius, the eye of the Great Dog.

I remembered Jack Pepper waiting, his glossy nose against the pane of glass at the shop, the expectation in his eyes that I would return. Was he still waiting for me? I wanted to reach out and hook that star right under my arm and carry it back with me. But that star didn't move either.

I went home. Kirsty and Milly had drawn posters. I wrote on them, "Please help us find Jack Pepper." Words helped George; they were like a key to make him feel good. But they were hopeless black marks on paper to me.

Everyone in our house went to bed. I should have gone too. But I walked the streets. I stuck the posters up until Jack Pepper shined in the copper beams of every lamppost on our road.

Nineteen

I was still in bed, trying to forget, to fill the hole in me with sleep, but I couldn't find much of that either. Kirsty and Milly were hovering in the doorway.

"Leo, you have to get up," Kirsty said. "School's canceled because of the sinkhole, but you're not going to find Jack Pepper lying there."

I'd tried to find Jack in my dreams. I tried to bring him back with my imagination. But it was no use. He wasn't really there. I didn't want to think about Grizzly anymore. I saw Jupiter, giant like a mountain, and the audience outside my window, leaning in, bearing down on me, Jupiter's outstretched thumb about to crush me. The lion trembling as Jupiter held him back.

"Did anyone call after seeing the posters?" I said.

"We've had a few calls," Kirsty said, "but it's only people asking if he's the little dog from town, Grizzly's dog. Nobody's seen him, but they're all going to look in their garages and sheds and under their hedges."

"You should keep looking, Leo," Milly said.

"You should go to all the places Jack Pepper has been before," Kirsty said. "Where else did you take him?"

Everything I'd done, all of it, including going to the Rec, made me feel small and weak.

"I'll stay here in case anyone else rings," Kirsty said. "Now get up, Leo; anyone would think you don't care."

"I do!" I yelled, throwing back the covers. "More than you understand." Jack was my partner, my lion in the amphitheater. He made me feel strong. It was all down to him. Not me.

"What don't I understand?" Kirsty said.

She had no idea about all the events, the truth that led up to this. Nobody did. How did wanting to be a hero turn out like this?

"It's all my fault," I moaned, flopping back down heavily, hiding my face in my hands.

"Then do something about it," Kirsty said. "Or can't you do anything unless Warren Miller says so?"

"It's nothing to do with him," I said quickly. "Why did you even mention him?"

"He called." She left that hanging in the air with a question in her eyebrows, as if she had more information than she was letting on.

"What did he say?"

"He said he'd seen you with Jack." Was she deliberately leaving big gaps between her words?

"What else?"

"He said . . . Jack was scared of you."

"That's not true!" I said.

I couldn't defend myself. I was too afraid I'd let the whole story slip out.

"He had no right to say that."

Kirsty frowned. She went downstairs, taking Milly with her. I heard Milly say, "What's happened to Leo?"

* * *

The recreation field was a big open space edged by the old Roman wall, so I knew straightaway that Jack wasn't there because there was nowhere to hide. I had to go back there though, to the places we'd been together. I was looking around the bike park in case Jack was hiding behind the half pipe, when Warren Miller and his friends arrived and skidded around me on their bikes.

"Sad about you losing your bike, Leo," Warren said. "How's old Grizzly Allen?"

I felt my jaw tighten. Warren's eyes narrowed. Was he threatening me? Showing me he was in control of the truth? Why mention Grizzly? I didn't think Warren knew him.

"Why did you tell my sister that Jack Pepper was scared of me?" I said.

He shrugged, like he couldn't see why I was getting angry about something like that.

"That's what it looked like to me," he said, and I took a step forward, thinking about punching him, but he was much bigger than me and there were too many other people.

"Leo, Leo," Warren said, all calm and in control, showing that sharp tooth under his crooked lip. "We miss you, buddy. We want you with us, not against us. Why don't you have a go on my bike? Try it out if you want."

I was stunned for a moment when Warren got off his bike and held the handlebars out to me.

"Come on," he said. "We're still friends, aren't we? Have a go. I bet you miss your bike, don't you?"

I couldn't work out what was going on; my head wasn't clear. I remembered Grizzly saying if you're going to fight you needed to think straight.

"Come with us," Warren said. "You can borrow it."

And you know what? I thought of Jack Pepper twisting and turning right beside me, like he was part of me, stuck to me whatever I did. Right then I remembered that little white dog running across the Rec. Toward me. I wondered for the first time: Did he think . . . did he think I would save him back then?

"Ten minutes," Warren said. "Then we'll help you find the stupid dog, won't we, guys?"

I took in a breath, but I couldn't say anything. I'd already called the dog stupid in front of him. I'd made this as bad as it was.

"Come on, you're not choosing that mutt over us,

are you? The dog can wait ten minutes."

My stomach tensed with knowing I'd already asked Jack to wait outside the shop. I felt the sky rumbling with a new audience, stamping their feet as Jupiter drummed his great impatient fingers. Think!

"Yes," I said, "I'm choosing Jack Pepper."

Twenty

There was a silence I'd never heard before on Great Western Road. There were no cars, buses, or trucks, no dull hum of our town or the people. The traffic had been diverted. Shopkeepers and shoppers, a few dozen people who would have been on North Road, were being kept away by the barriers. They stood staring with the police, who had their backs to the disaster behind them. They were all at least a hundred yards away from the sinkhole and nobody was allowed through.

I kept on walking to the barriers. There was only one place that Jack could be.

"Jack Pepper's down that sinkhole!" I shouted to

a policeman. "You have to get him out!"

Radios crackled; messages were relayed. The words rippled through the people. Someone was missing; someone was unaccounted for.

"We thought everyone was safe."

"Jack Pepper? We know that name."

The policeman let me through. He rushed me closer, over to the fire engines. I could see the dark rim of the sinkhole now, the huge open space where cars and buses and trucks used to make their way across the center of our town. Layers of asphalt and stone and earth, the crust of the ground that had gone.

More police and rescue services gathered round me.

"When did you last see Jack?"

"Are you sure? Have you checked?"

"He hasn't gone home, he was here in town," I said.

"How old is Jack Pepper?"

"About three years old," I said.

"Call in a search and rescue team!"

"We need heat-sensing equipment!"

There was worry and urgency in their voices.

They hadn't secured the surrounding buildings yet. They didn't know what they were dealing with; the ground was unsteady, whatever was under there, unknown.

"Where are Jack's parents?" the policeman asked. "Why aren't they here?"

"A three-year-old boy has fallen down the sinkhole!"

"It's not a boy," I told them. "Jack Pepper's a dog."

Radios crackled. The activity calmed.

"It's just a dog," a fireman said into his radio.

"He's not just a dog!" I shouted, because I knew what he meant. "If you knew . . . if you saw Grizzly's face when I didn't bring Jack back . . ." I could hardly speak. "Please, he's just as important as anyone else around here."

And more important than me.

The fireman put a gloved hand on my shoulder, led me back to the barriers. I looked at the fireman's uniform. That meant he could rescue people. Surely he could rescue dogs too.

"You can save him. I can't."

"Son, we can't go sending crew down that hole just yet, not at risk to their own lives. Not for somebody's dog. Are you sure he's down there?"

"I've looked everywhere; he's nowhere else. What if he is down there? What if he's hurt and waiting for someone to come and rescue him?"

And then I wish I hadn't said it because I could see the hopelessness of a small dog stuck in the rubble reflected in that fireman's eyes.

I held his arms so he could see into my eyes, how serious I was.

"You have to get him out."

"Son." He knelt on one knee. "We've got a lot of work to do first. It's lucky nobody's been hurt. We've got the best possible people coming to make everything safe and sound. And, when that's done, I promise you, as soon as we can secure the area, we'll send someone down that hole for the dog."

He opened the barrier and firmly guided me back, pushing me toward the people who wanted to know more.

"Who's missing?"

"Who's unaccounted for?"

"Jack Pepper," I said, hanging my head.

"Grizzly Allen's dog?"

"That nice little dog a boy saved from the pond?"

"The one on the posters down our road?"

Someone recognized me. "It's Leo Biggs, isn't it? Ben's boy. You're the one who saved him before."

It didn't feel like praise anymore. They patted my shoulder, they smiled with their mouths, but their breath was full of sighs and their eyes full of sadness.

Nobody had questioned the holes in my story about my bike and the cat because I think everyone wanted to believe in heroes and something good happening.

"Aren't they going to do anything?" It was George, standing beside Beatrix. He barely looked at me, but he went up to the barriers and asked the fireman, "How long will it take?"

"We're working as quickly as we can," he said.

"Today? Tomorrow?" George asked. "When?"

"We're doing the best we can."

"And if there was a boy down there?" Beatrix asked. "Would you do better?"

There was no answer to Beatrix's question, only the promise of as soon as we can.

"Thanks," I said to George and Beatrix.

"We're not here for you," Beatrix said. "We're here for the dog."

They stood together, shoulder to shoulder. George wouldn't look directly at me. I lost a dog that stood by me. I lost my best friend who probably would have stood by me if I'd told him the truth.

"Mr. Allen asked me to come and find you; he wants to talk to you," George said. "Have you told him his dog might be down there?" He didn't wait for an answer. He moved away with Beatrix, as if we had nothing to do with each other.

Grizzly was hanging over his gate, his head drooping, turned a little just to let me know he knew I was coming.

"You'd better come in before one of us changes his mind," Grizzly said.

I stood there for an age by Grizzly's gate and tried to imagine time rewinding, to see Jack Pepper there again and things turning out differently. But it didn't work. It couldn't work.

Grizzly held the door open, stood back, let me in. I saw him dreading it as much as I was. I wasn't exactly sure what he wanted to say to me, why he was waiting, but it felt like a ton of bricks was hovering, about to tumble.

Jack's empty bed was still in front of the coal fire, no lights on, curtains half drawn, an uneasy flicker of light from the dying flames, two mugs of tea on the mantelpiece.

"Been looking out for you," Grizzly rumbled. "Saw you coming down the road. Had a brew ready. One of them's for you."

We took our time, sat, nervously tested the tea. I wished I had something hopeful to tell him, but the best I could do was to say that we'd made posters. Kirsty and Milly had drawn them and I'd put them up.

"I saw them. Very nice. Good likeness."

Heavy silence. We sipped our tea.

"I've been looking," I said, but it didn't sound like my voice. It was just words, filling the space, the cavern of emptiness we were in, the muddle of lies I was tangled up with. "But I think . . . I think . . . I know where he is."

Grizzly's hands shook. He spilled his tea. He put his mug down, wiped at his trouser leg.

"I told you about that fight I had with Nicky Sullivan, didn't I?" I nodded, grateful for the distraction, as every word I'd said was like a jab to our chests.

"I was an eighteen-year-old kid at Sullivan's club, sparring on a Friday night. Nicky used to put on his big championship belt with the shiny gold buckle for us and we'd get swept up in the glory of it all. I tried it on once, thought I'd like it to fit me." A smile flickered across his face. "Nicky saw me in the ring, said I'd make a good boxer. He asked me to stay behind late that night, spar a few rounds with him. There was just him and me and his manager. And a girl. The cleaner."

I imagined him then, younger, with fuller hair and livelier flesh, like a lean gladiator.

Grizzly shook his head like he decided it wasn't worth telling me any more. He laughed sadly at himself. "I'm too old to get up and fight these days. Not like you. You're just beginning to see the fights you might have to take on. And I don't mean in the ring."

The responsibility of still being seen as a hero by Grizzly was too much, but I knew then that I couldn't tell him what I'd done, ever, not even if I wanted to. There's only so much disappointment a person can feel. And then, in the silence that followed, the weight of knowing that neither Grizzly nor I wanted to admit that Jack Pepper was down that sinkhole caved me in. The smoke from the fire got in my eyes.

"Fights aren't necessarily what you have with fists or swords," Grizzly said, his voice so low I could feel it vibrating in my chest. "Sometimes we're just trying to put things right. On the inside. And it's not right that you're giving up on yourself. Because I can see that's what you're doing.

"I'm telling you now, Leo, I'll fight and Lucy . . . my girl . . . will fight too, to forgive what's happened to Jack. That's what I've always taught her to do. And you have to fight not to blame yourself or let this change you into someone else, someone who won't fight. We've all seen the hero in you, Leo lad."

He picked up the teapot, poured some more tea in our mugs.

"Lucy's going to be back in a few days," he said as if he was talking to himself, preparing himself to tell her what had happened. "Now drink your tea before it gets cold. You need your strength. You're not fighting in your dreams anymore. You're fighting to keep your heart as good and whole as it should be."

Twenty-One

George was by himself, waiting down the road for me. I couldn't take anyone else telling me how disappointed in me they were. I already knew. If he'd known, he'd have told me every good reason why I shouldn't have gone to the recreation field to meet Warren Miller and his friends that night in the first place.

That's the thing about friends: they see the things in you that you don't like either, not because they think badly of you, but because they believe much better of you. But I knew that had all gone now. George and Beatrix didn't think anything good about me anymore. I didn't deserve any friends, even though I wanted them back.

I wanted Jack back most of all though, because I truly believed he was the only one that could make everything right again. Just being near George made me feel worse about what I'd done to Grizzly and Jack Pepper. I walked past him.

"I've been thinking," George said. "Jack Pepper is most likely to be down the sinkhole."

I stopped and turned around.

"Do you think I don't know that?"

"Beatrix thinks he's down there too."

"I know, George, you don't need to rub it in."

I walked away.

"I'm only telling you because we believe he's still alive," George called.

That stunned me because that's what I felt deep inside, or had to believe. There was something that was part of me, still beating, still hoping, still fighting, needing this to turn out right. But I didn't dare wish.

Mostly I believed Jack Pepper was in the sinkhole because I couldn't imagine the goodness in him gone for good.

"He would have waited outside the shop, because

I asked him to," I said. I didn't say what that might mean if he was down there. I had nothing but hope keeping him alive in me. And it didn't feel like enough. I needed someone else to believe he was alive too. I needed George to believe.

"How long can a dog survive without food or water?" I asked, because George was the one who always knew the answers.

"Depends," George said. "I looked it up and you have to consider all the circumstances. The weather, how old Jack is; he's young, so that's quite good. Also if he's injured . . ." He caught my eye for a second and knew not to say any more. "Probably three days at most, in these conditions. It's really cold."

I nodded, turned to go, thinking how little time the emergency services had to rescue Jack.

"Mr. Allen asked me to do something else for him," George called, but I was already running down the road. I didn't want to listen. I had to do something, ask the rescue services again. I had to get some help. I ran back to the barriers on Great Western, but I was told to step back, to leave the professionals to get on with their job. Frustration and a whole heap of other things rose in me like I wanted to roar, but it wouldn't come out.

George had followed me. He put a hand on my shoulder and I turned around.

"I promised Mr. Allen I'd help you," George said. "But this doesn't mean we're friends."

It was the killer blow, even though I didn't deserve George as a friend anyway. I knew then that Jack Pepper had followed me to the pond that day. He was trying to stop me getting into trouble, just like George would have done. I'd lost George as a friend now, so it wouldn't matter what he thought of me, but I couldn't stand lying to him anymore and how that was eating me up inside. I grabbed his arm and dragged him away from the other people.

"I didn't rescue Jack Pepper from the pond," I told him. "He was trying to rescue me, George. Me!"

George turned his back for a second. I could hear him breathing, big angry breaths through his nose.

"You wouldn't understand, George." But I couldn't find the right words to explain why.

He marched away.

"You have to make this right, Leo!" he shouted.

"I know! But I can't!"

My voice was lost, like something small in a dark pit, and before I had the chance to say anything else, George turned back and said, "I do understand! You wanted to be a gladiator, to be a hero. So stop pretending. It's about time you really were one."

Twenty-Two

I dreamed I was digging in a sand dune, desperate to find a bone that Jack Pepper had buried somewhere and was lost. I kept digging because I knew if I found the bone then I'd find him. But the sand pile got bigger and bigger and slipped away in my hands, and I was hiding from the lion, but I knew he was there, behind the dune, about to find me. And then I was falling and falling.

"Leo?" It was Dad, his voice soft. I woke with a jump. "You're all right, son. You're in the living room, safe, at home."

I opened my eyes, not sure where I was.

"Was he sleepwalking?" Milly said.

"I think he was trying to find Jack Pepper," Dad said.

I was lying by the fireplace, in pajamas and shoes and a coat.

I rubbed my hands over my face. There was coal dust on my palms. My hands were black. There was ash and soot all over the hearth.

"What time is it?" I asked.

"Seven o'clock," Dad said. "There's no school. With the roads out and all the cars and buses diverted, nobody's going in again today."

That's not what I was thinking. I was wondering how many hours Jack Pepper had been down the hole. Was he still alive? Alone. Hurt? Still waiting for me? Something was different today though. I was carrying him, somewhere inside of me. I felt stronger, and I wasn't going to let him go.

"I've got to go back to the sinkhole," I told Dad.

I washed off the soot, put on some clothes. Dad caught me in the kitchen when I didn't eat the pile of toast he'd made.

"Leo, I just want you to know that I'm proud of you, son."

"Yeah, Dad."

"I mean it. Look at me, Leo. . . . I'm proud of what you did before and I'm proud of what you're doing now to try to find Jack. I didn't realize a little dog like that might mean so much to you."

"No, Dad."

Someone else I couldn't ever tell, not now. I already knew what it was like to lose pride in yourself. I'd let so many people down even though they might not know it, and I couldn't do that to Dad.

"Whatever happens, nobody's going to blame you, Leo. Jack falling into the hole wasn't your fault."

I wondered, did it matter what anybody else thought of me when I thought nothing of myself?

I was the first one at the barriers, the first person to watch and hope and believe that the emergency services would find Jack down there. People slowly joined me, lined up along the barriers, rubbing their arms against the cold.

We exchanged something, with every new person that arrived, a message in our eyes that we were all here for a good reason. We were all useless because we couldn't help, but we were all fighting on the inside for Jack Pepper.

"Any news?" someone asked as a policeman came up to the barriers.

"Anyone found that lovely little dog?"

"Is anyone looking for Jack Pepper yet?" I said.

"They will," he said. In the meantime, all we could do was wait. All of us willing good news, all of us standing vigil over the sinkhole.

News rippled through. Someone had heard that a crane was coming this way, but was stuck on North Road because cracks had appeared. They had to stop and put up scaffolding first to make the buildings safe.

There were dozens of people in uniform between the barriers and the hole. Scaffolding was also being put up round a building on Great Western, two doors up from the dress shop. That's how close they were to making it safe enough to climb down into the hole and search for Jack Pepper. But it might just as well have been a mile away.

The hours trudged by while we watched the slow progress as more scaffolding went up.

There was a commotion at the edge of the crowd, the smell of a familiar ingredient. It was my dad, loaded up with bags of chips and boxes of fried chicken.

"Help yourselves," Dad said, offering them around. "You need to keep your strength up."

Dad was happiest when he was filling someone else's belly. People offered him money, but he said, "Put it in the charity box; there's always someone else who needs it more."

People passed the food along to the emergency services, handed it out to everyone and anyone who wanted it. Kirsty came with a shopping cart filled with paper cups of tea and milk and sugar for anyone who needed warmth inside them. Mom and Milly carried a bag of bottles of juice and plastic cups for the children.

I thought of Grizzly then, how he said we all needed our bodies fed and fit for fighting. I could almost feel the strength of everyone growing in the smell of fried chicken, all of us fighting inside for things to turn out right, for Jack Pepper to be found, bright and alive.

"Dad said you didn't eat your breakfast," Kirsty said.

"I wasn't hungry. I can't stop thinking about Jack Pepper," I said quietly.

"None of us are giving up," she said. "We should think of him, and we should send him our thoughts, and we just keep holding on like that."

"I don't see how that helps," I said.

"What else can we do?" she said through her teeth.

Kirsty stared at me like she had something else to say, but couldn't bring herself to say it. She turned away. Even my sister thought what Warren had said about me was true. Even she believed that I had scared Jack, and she'd known me all my life.

"I'm going home to check the phone," Kirsty said. "Just in case someone has found Jack and called."

Time is the most uncomfortable thing in the world, when there's nothing you can do.

A mountain search and rescue team arrived in a van. They appeared like real hope in orange jackets, with ropes and clips and hard hats and other equipment. We all pushed closer to the barriers, huddled and pressed against each other, but the police moved us away from the team, gave them room. This was the first movement we'd seen from our end of the street, the first time someone really looked like they were going to do something.

"Are you going to get our dog?" I said, clinging to the barrier. Our dog. Not Grizzly's dog, not Lucy's. Ours because everyone standing nearby was there for the same reason.

I called to the rescue team. "He's been down there for more than two days. Please, get him out!"

"We'll do what we can," one of them said.

People blew on their hands and stamped their feet against the bitter day. I couldn't think about how cold Jack Pepper might be or that he wasn't alive. I just thought and hoped and told him inside, *You hold on, Jack, just wait a little bit longer. Someone's coming.* But I didn't understand why the emergency services were just standing around and talking.

The minutes ticked past like dripping molasses. Machines humming and buzzing, people murmuring and sighing. People talked about Grizzly, how long they'd known him, stories from the past. They all knew something about each other. The stories were good: they were about the good things in all of us. And I felt left out because all I'd been doing lately was telling lies.

Police radios crackled. We heard that a huge digger was now trying to approach the sinkhole from the other end of North Road.

A policeman got a message through his radio. I saw him scanning the crowd, picking me out. I saw he wished he hadn't caught my eye, and he turned away.

I ran over. "What?" I said. "What do you know?"

I saw him take a breath, wrestling with himself whether to tell me or not.

"It's about the dog," he said. "Well, we don't know for sure, and I don't want to get anybody's hopes up. . . ."

People surged forward to hear, a murmur of expectation.

The policeman blew out his cheeks, took another deep breath.

"The heat-sensing equipment shows blues and greens where it's cold, reds and yellows if there's body heat, if there's someone there, if they're . . ." He breathed, crouched, and pulled me closer. "There's a faint yellow glow coming from the sinkhole. It might be the dog."

People cried and laughed, held on to each other,

shook hands, patted each other's backs, held back their smiles. All I could do right then was try to breathe and stand upright.

Words rippled through the crowd.

"Is it the dog?"

"Is it that little Jack Pepper?"

"Is he alive?"

There was so much commotion, so much hope.

Then a roar of voices.

The front of the building that was next to the dress shop crumbled.

Tumbled.

Collapsed.

Smashed into the hole.

More dust, more running. Engines started up; fire engines moved back. The police ducked under the barriers; even the people behind them took a step away. The ground wasn't safe.

I didn't move. I couldn't move, trying so hard to will this not to be happening.

"Stop!" I shouted. "You're supposed to be getting closer! You're supposed to be finding the dog!" Words were no use. People started to leave.

Then the search and rescue team came running

back, with their ropes and clips and hard hats.

"Where are you going?" I said, stirred and angry that they were leaving. I jumped in front of them. "There's a yellow glow; he's down there. You have to go back and get Jack Pepper out!"

One of them looked back as the dust blossomed in the street from the spilled and smashed building.

"Sorry, son," he said. Another hand on my shoulder. "Nobody's going to be a hero today."

Twenty-Three

The night swooped in. Everybody left except me.

"Go home, son," a policeman said. "There's nothing you can do standing here."

The emergency services packed up, said they needed to go away to regroup, rethink, plan their next move. Everyone abandoned the sinkhole and what was in it to go home, to sleep, to sigh, to pray, to wish and warm themselves.

Another slow day had gone past too quickly.

George once told me that he read in a book that where we live the earth is rotating at about six hundred and fifty miles an hour. He'd said that, if the earth suddenly stopped spinning, the atmosphere would keep going and pretty much everything would be scoured off the planet. I sat on a wall on Clarendon Road and imagined buildings, cars, people, everything in the street, everything in our houses, all the bikes from TrailBlaze sucked into the atmosphere, to spin and float around Earth like an asteroid belt.

I watched the sky. Jupiter stuck out his foot, stopped the earth from spinning, held on to us like a football.

The earth threw everything up in the air: the rubble, the shop, everything that collapsed into the sinkhole. Including Jack Pepper. Then we were like astronauts, spacemen, swimming without gravity. I didn't look twice at any bike from TrailBlaze. I took giant leaps to Jack Pepper, Jupiter smiling down, kicking aside any meteors and asteroids in our way with his giant foot. He laughed like thunder as I hooked Jack under my arm and showed him Sirius.

"See that star, that burning light, that brightest star? That's you, Jack Pepper."

We floated and swam in space some more to find Grizzly . . . then I was going to hand Jack back so the cave in our hearts wouldn't be empty anymore.

My neck ached from looking up, wishing Jupiter and his mighty fist or foot would get Jack out, or the archer, the charioteer, the bear, any of them, would do something. But I didn't have any control over the way things really were.

"Wishing is for stupid people!" I shouted to them. "I wished for a bike for my birthday, that's all, and now look what's happened!"

The gods and creatures were all fake, all hanging there and not able to do anything, not answer, not help. They looked like statues: gray, solid, pointless. We were all like statues.

"And what's the point of imagining things?" I told them. "What's your imagination even for? It just lets you down in the end."

I grabbed my head in my hands, as if that would help wipe them all away. "You're not real! You're . . . you're just explosions from millions of years ago."

I slid off the wall and kicked a can in the road.

"That's real! It's solid and you can kick it!" I paced up and down and kept shouting—at nothing. My voice echoed off the houses. "Real Romans left behind real things! Things that are now buried underground because they're so old. . . ."

Underground! My voice echoed off the walls. Underground! The emergency services were all trying to get into the hole from above, where buildings were falling down, where they couldn't get close. Why hadn't they tried to go underground?

I ran to George's. I didn't know what else to do.

George looked surprised when he opened the door.

"I need your help. Please, George."

He flinched, took half a step back, as if he didn't trust me anymore.

"You said you'd help," I said. "I think I know what the emergency services need to do."

He let me in the hall, but no farther.

"Tomorrow Jack will have been down there for three nights, George." He took that in. So did I. "They can't get the crane close enough because the buildings aren't safe. There must be another way in."

There was a kind of calm that I hadn't felt before. Like clouds cleared from the sky. I thought about that day when I walked through town with Jack. Not so I could remember what people said about me. I didn't care about that anymore.

What I remembered was what Jack had done for everyone. No words, but just a minute with that dog looking into you with nothing but loyalty made us all feel good. And it was only a minute he spent with each person, but look how long it had lasted; look how big it had become.

Jack Pepper wasn't even as tall as my knee, but we'd all looked up to him.

"They'll have to clear the other rubble away first before they can get closer anyway." I saw George's shoulders relax. He was at his best when you asked him to help. "Come upstairs," he said. "I'll show you something."

We went to his bedroom and he unfolded a map and spread it out on the floor. Lines and words and symbols, a code for the ground.

"I've been studying this old map I got in the library yesterday." He ran his finger over the roads that he was talking about. "Look at this. See how straight this road is? I bet it was once a Roman road."

"You know you said there might be a river or something that had eroded the ground below the road, the reason the sinkhole collapsed? What else is underground around here?"

"I don't know," George said, looking at the symbol key, "but I could try to look it up."

I couldn't wait for George to find out more. I just looked at the map and knew there was more to our town than what was on the surface.

"What else could be under the shops and road?" I said. "Could somebody get to Jack from underground?"

Then I noticed that George's mom was outside the bedroom door. Her wary eyes flicked from me to George.

"Leo, leave this to the professionals. You've already proved you're a hero. There's no need to prove it again."

Every time someone called me a hero I felt empty inside.

"You'd better go. You can tell them about this tomorrow morning," George said. But not before he looked at me for a long time, then whispered, "You might need this," and his eyes were wide as he secretly shoved the map inside my coat pocket.

I couldn't sleep, thinking about what I should and shouldn't do. I looked out of the window at Sirius, hoping for an answer. I saw a light on farther down the road. Grizzly's house. I wondered what he was doing up. Was he thinking like I was? Not sleeping, but worrying about Jack Pepper.

The lion was outside my window, looking up at me, his strong shoulders flexing as he shifted his weight. I wiped the condensation away to see him more clearly. He turned and headed off toward the corner of Clarendon Road and Great Western. He watched me over his shoulder and I wanted to follow, just like Jack had tried to do.

I put my coat and shoes on over my pajamas and crept outside.

The frosty air bit at my nose and ears and hands. There was still an eerie silence because of all the vehicles that were missing from our streets. The barriers were still up, flashing beacons, danger signs. The lion went along the alleyway behind the empty lot where the shop had been pulled down last year. I saw him through the chicken wire, then he disappeared behind the lot, his shadow shrinking into a small catlike creature.

I headed down Great Western toward the sinkhole. Nobody was there. I ducked under the barriers, hugged the pavement in front of the shops until I stood behind more barriers, just yards from the sinkhole. It was darker there because the streetlights weren't working, ripped up, the wires snapped. There was only the flashing of the yellow roadwork lights. I crawled under the barriers, testing each foot and hand before I put my weight on them.

The hole was huge, about thirty yards across, but it was hard to tell how deep. The pavement stopped, a broken edge, darkness beyond.

I lay down, shuffled on my elbows, not knowing how safe the ground was underneath me, until I could peer over the edge.

The depth of gloom, the chaos of the rubble down there, scared me.

My eyes got used to the blackness. Loose fragments crumbled below me, scattered into the dark. I heard them land, bounce, rattle into the distant emptiness.

"Jack Pepper," I whispered. "Someone will come and get you."

I said his name over and over again. I rested my face on my arms, turned my head so my ear was listening down there. I whispered his name again and again. I thought he should hear me call. I thought he should know I was fighting.

I got up on my knees. In the sky, Jupiter hung there, hard and cold. There was no show for him to see. No hero to watch. It wasn't me who was the hero anyway.

I thought of all the people in our town helping to clear up the damage. My dad handing out food, the girls warming people with hot tea. All those people from our town sharing words of encouragement. I thought of Kirsty, sitting by the phone all day, waiting for news of Jack Pepper. I thought of Jack pulling me out of the pond.

They were all heroes in small but great ways.

Twenty-Four

I walked home again, willing the night to go quickly, for the emergency services to come back so I could tell them what George had found on the map. I couldn't go back to bed—that felt like giving up—so I sat outside our back door in the bitter night with the frost stinging my eyes.

The bathroom light came on upstairs, cast a beam over me. Then it went off. Then the hall light came on, then the kitchen light. The back door opened. Mom was in her dressing gown.

"What are you doing out here?" she said. "It's half past four in the morning."

"How did you know I was here?"

"I don't know. I saw your bed was empty . . . I don't know. I didn't know I'd find you here." She crouched down, ran her hand over my hair. "Oh, Leo. You mustn't blame yourself about Jack Pepper going missing."

But before she could say any more, neither of us could believe our eyes when someone else came through the back gate. Warren Miller. And he had my old bike.

Startled to see us, he hesitated. Whatever he was doing, he hadn't expected to see us either. His eyes looked like they were searching, looking for the best possible outcome from this situation.

"Leo? What's going on?" Mom said. "And who are you? What are you doing here at this hour of the morning?"

All I did was take a breath. Warren Miller wasn't only big, he was a quicker thinker than me.

"I couldn't sleep, not after what happened. I got Leo's bike out of the pond," he said. "Even though I didn't agree with what he did—"

"Mom, don't listen to him!"

"Leo, let him finish. What didn't you agree with?"

"I don't want to get Leo in trouble and I really

didn't want to say anything, but it's been bothering me a lot, Mrs. Biggs."

"What has?"

"Mom, please—" I tried to interrupt. He was lying!

Then he told her everything. Well, his version. That I'd sunk Grizzly Allen's scooter in the pond at the recreation field because I was trying to impress everyone. He said I'd tripped Mr. Patterson because I hated doing presentations. That I had chased Grizzly's dog, but he wasn't sure why. That I'd fallen in the pond, not dived in, and lost my bike in there.

The dog didn't go in the pond. It was too scared of me, he said. And he was sorry that he hadn't said anything sooner, but he couldn't keep it to himself any longer.

I didn't have a whisper of strength to fight back.

Mom straightened her back. "Stay here," she said. "Both of you. I need to get your father, Leo."

I looked up at Warren. It was pointless trying to defend what I'd done and all I could think was that if I gave my version of what happened it would just sound like I was trying to cover up my part in it and make me look even more guilty.

"Why are you doing this?" I said.

"I've got plans for you." Warren smiled his lop-sided smile. "You'll thank me in the end."

"Plans?"

"You'll see."

It all made sense now. Warren didn't need a gladiator.

"You need someone stupid like me to take the blame for you," I said.

"We all need a fall guy," he said. "Yours was the dog."

I shook my head. Numb. With cold, with guilt. He was right though: I'd used Jack Pepper to get myself out of trouble and to make people believe I was something that I wasn't.

I heard voices, all of my family coming to the door.

The light from the kitchen faded as Dad filled the doorway. Mom and the girls pressed at his back to find a gap to see from behind him. A different wave of panic and hurt cut into me when I saw the pride gone from Dad's questioning face and the disappointment left there.

"He hurt Jack Pepper," I said, pointing at Warren, but Warren was too clever for me.

"It was an accident," Warren said, his voice higher pitched, trembling at the sight of my dad. "I feel really bad. But it was an accident, just like Leo's accident with Mr. Patterson." He was far too clever for me, spinning the story to make himself look good—which was what I'd done too.

"I only came to bring Leo's bike back because I was sorry for him that he didn't have it anymore and couldn't come out with us. I even had to go in the pond to get it."

Slowly I shook my head. It was even worse than I thought when he said it out loud. And he and his friends were right: all I had to do was get rid of Grizzly's scooter and I'd be like them.

"Does your dad know you're here?" Dad said to Warren.

"No." Warren twitched.

"Then I suggest you go on in the kitchen and wait for me."

Warren stepped over me.

"Go to your room, Leo," Dad said. "We've got a lot of talking to do."

Twenty-Five

I heard someone sit against the back of my bedroom door. They sighed, then went away again.

Then I heard whispering. The floorboards outside my door creaked.

"Go on," Milly whispered.

"All right, all right," Kirsty whispered back.

I heard moving around downstairs, then the girls' footsteps running and Milly's bedroom door closing. A few minutes later the girls came back.

"I don't believe the things Warren said," Kirsty whispered through the door. "Tell me the truth. What really happened?"

"I didn't mean to hurt Grizzly," I whispered. "Why would I do that? He was good to me—he tried to fix my bike." I put my face by the crack of the door. "I didn't know it was his mobility scooter. I wouldn't have done it if I'd known."

Whispering.

"Does that mean you would have done it if it was somebody else's, not Grizzly's?" Kirsty said.

"I know it was wrong," I said. "I hate that I did it and I wish . . ." What was the point of wishing? I started to think I wouldn't have done it if Warren and his friends hadn't cheered me and lied to me. But that wasn't true. I wanted to be somebody worthwhile, to feel brave like a gladiator, but I'd gotten it all wrong.

"I shouldn't have done it," I said. "If I could take it all back, I would. . . ."

I had to tell someone the truth.

"I got scared. . . ." All my pride was defeated now. I whispered, "I got scared because I wasn't anybody special. And I lied about what happened because I thought it wouldn't matter if people thought I was the hero, not Jack."

The girls were quiet for a minute.

I waited, and then Milly said, "You made me not scared of the meteor, Leo. You said it was going to burn bright and I'd like it. And I did, except not what happened to Jack Pepper."

All I could think then was that Jack needed a gladiator on his side to protect him, and it was going to have to be me.

"I'm going to put this all right again," I said. "I need your help though."

Kirsty took a big breath. "What do you want us to do?"

Twenty-Six

Kirsty kept a lookout and Milly made sure Mom and Dad stayed in the kitchen. I didn't have time to think or care about what they were saying.

"Don't do anything stupid," Kirsty whispered as I crept down the stairs. "Good luck."

I slipped out of the front door and ran all the way to the sinkhole.

I put on my gladiator helmet, took up a stance, and wielded my pretend shield to the sky. Jupiter looked amused. He shifted his toga on his shoulder, stroked the lion at his side. I could hear them, the audience, the amphitheater filling again, murmuring with the expectation of life and death. And even though I knew that they were just in my imagination, what I was about to do was not. I threw down the helmet. I wasn't going to be blindsided this time. This battle was going to take place in the real world, and I had to win.

The ground trembled. Bulldozers were coming from the far side of Great Western Road, their headlights roaming the ground.

I ducked behind the barriers.

I heard a voice. "Whoa!" A man in a fluorescent jacket and hard hat stood before the bulldozers, waving his arms. The engines slowed and rumbled.

"Knock down those first two buildings on the left. We'll use the rubble to start filling up the hole."

They were going to bury Jack! Think! There must be a way to get underground. What did I know? And then I remembered the cellar in the dress shop.

I ran back down the road until I came to the back of the dress shop. The back wall was still standing, like the fragile skin of the shop that had once been there. The back door sagged on a broken hinge. I shoved it aside and wished I hadn't. I heard the dry bricks slipping like a cough against each other, the scatter of debris. I ducked, wrapped my arms over my head to escape the small landslide. The noise, the movement, the avalanche stopped. I shook off the dust.

The front of the shop had gone, but the steps to the cellar still led down into the dark.

The cellar was heavy with dead silence, but smelled of new things. The painted stone walls were hidden by racks of clothes. The closest wall to the sinkhole was straight ahead of me.

I felt around, felt the scratch of dust in my hands, the way the floor sloped away. I slid down, kicked out because I couldn't see clearly what was in front of me. Then I kicked against stones, fallen stones, and a gap! The corner of the cellar had fallen away and there was a hole. A small hole, big enough for maybe a cat, but not for me. I felt air, like a cold breath, coming through it.

I pulled apart one of the clothes rails to get at a metal tube. I hammered at the stone wall with it. I smashed and smashed those stones until they loosened like old teeth. I kicked them away until the hole was big enough for me to climb through.

A new smell gushed out. Like the smell in a

museum, ancient, preserved, musty, but the hole fell away into nothing but deeper darkness. What if it was too deep? What if I fell and couldn't get back up?

I crouched and slumped against the stones, steadied my breath and trembling hands. I felt how alone I was without my audience in the sky. How could I stand up and do something brave if nobody saw, if nobody was watching?

But I couldn't rely on them anymore, even if they cheered. They were in my imagination, and so was the gladiator I used to be.

Then I thought of the real people that mattered. My family. George. Grizzly. Jack Pepper, alone too in the dark. It was him I wanted to be like.

I filled my lungs with air, climbed into the hole, let my weight hang from my arms. They stretched and strained. I let go.

My feet hit the ground not far below, but I crumpled as my ankles twisted and rolled.

There's nothing wrong with darkness, I told myself. It's exactly the same as when it's light, except, because we can't see, we imagine the things we're scared of. They loomed in my head: the bear, the tiger, and the lion. And the real things: being nobody worthwhile.

I reached out. A wall curved up and away from me, built with what felt like large bricks. A breeze touched my right cheek. I looked that way, saw the palest glimmer of hope in a yellowy light. My eyes adjusted.

I could soon make out why the walls curved away above and beside me when I found myself in a passageway, surrounded by arches and pillars and small rooms like cells. I'd seen pictures like this in a book. The cells and cages of the gladiators and wild animals that would take center stage lay beneath the arena floor. Was I in the underground section of a Roman amphitheater?

Is that why dreams of gladiators and the arena were so vivid to me? Was it because our town was built within Roman walls along arrow-straight roads that made me imagine the gladiator in me, with the sand of the amphitheater beneath my feet? Touching the earth where battles had once been. I wondered, could something abandoned for hundreds and hundreds of years seep through the earth? Could the spirit of the gladiator have gotten into my dreams and imagination? Into me?

At the end of the passageway the light was stronger, but still pale and dim. I began to stumble, feel rubble under my feet, the crunch of sand and small stones. More rubble that I had to climb over, until I reached the end of the passage and was standing below an arch. The archway was blocked almost to the top by the debris of fallen buildings, apart from a small space of pale light.

I started to climb, pushing my hands and feet deep into the rubble, but it was like a steep sand dune: there was nothing holding it all together. Stones clattered and fell away into the darkness. Things slipped from underneath me.

I slid. Nothing I could feel belonged down there. It wasn't smooth or soft or stable. I grabbed out for something to hold on to until I found a narrow beam of concrete wedged into the side of the sinkhole. I pulled myself up on it. Above me, through the top of the archway, the asphalt crust was dark, lit only by a glimmer of hope from a bright star.

I called out, "Jack Pepper!"

My voice started something. Pieces of rubble clinked and clattered and echoed farther down, where it was darker and blacker. I kept still, clinging to the concrete, because it seemed like the only solid thing down there.

"Jack!" I whispered.

I lay along the concrete, let my arms hang, and reached into the dust. I scratched the surface of the pile. I buried my hands, dug with my fingers, grazing my knuckles, pushing away small pieces of brick and stone and earth. I only looked up once, to see how enormous the hole was, how the things I moved away might be burying Jack even further. I didn't let myself think it was impossible. I kept digging.

I touched something soft. Fur.

"I'm coming, Jack!" I called.

I leaped back onto the heap. I dug, faster, pushing away the rubble with my forearms, fighting against what was slipping down from above me, anchoring my knees again and again as they slid away. I felt the fur. I held on tight, pulled and pulled.

The rubble crumbled, fell away. I slipped. It wasn't a dog in my hands. It was a fake fur coat.

Twenty-Seven

T hunder rumbled closer. The bulldozers were coming. How long did I have until they demolished the surrounding buildings and filled in the sinkhole like a grave?

I panicked, kicked and clawed at the rubble nearest me. It felt useless. Pointless. It was dim down there, although my eyes had adjusted. All I saw was the jagged edge of the mountain of rubble, piled up through the archway. Did I really think I could find Jack Pepper in there?

I wished George was here to help me, to look up the answer in a book. How do you find a dog in a sinkhole full of rubble? I shivered, the deathly cold and fear prickling my skin. I picked up the coat, put it on to protect me, sank to the ground, pressed my head in my hands. I wanted to shout. To tell someone up there to get me out. I wanted somebody to come and rescue me. But I couldn't let that happen again, and it wouldn't. Nobody knew I was here.

The thundering of the bulldozers grew louder.

I shouted, yelled, roared.

But what was that other noise?

"Jack Pepper!" I called, making a cone around my mouth.

I closed my eyes to help me hear. But the rumbling grew.

"Jack Pepper!"

Was that him? A whimper. Had I imagined it?

"It's me, boy! Where are you?"

But the growl of those bulldozers vibrated right through me, shaking at the debris, quaking the ground, drowning out other sounds. Rubble slipped away from the arch; lights roamed the rim; fragments of buildings came tumbling in.

I scrabbled up the bank, slipping again, trying to cling to things that were not steady or stable. I dug in, climbed my way up to the top of the arch where I thought I'd heard Jack.

My hands tore at the stones and concrete and brick, throwing them down behind me. Did I hear Jack growl? Was it my imagination or an echo of the bulldozers rumbling above my head?

I dug and dug where I thought the sound had come from until I found a space under the beam of concrete big enough to put my arm through. I stretched, reached in, pushed my shoulder against the slab, but it wouldn't budge. I kicked and kicked away at the crumbling parts. Reached in again, pushed my arm until I felt something soft. Jack's ear! Jack's collar! I hooked one finger in just as the boom of another huge pile of rubble landed in the sinkhole.

Big dull thuds of brick and concrete clattered above me. Thunder vibrated through me. The pile shifted, falling back. The collar slipped from my fingers and I couldn't feel Jack Pepper anymore. The debris collapsed like sand as more rubble was pushed into the hole by the diggers. I'd had him and now I didn't.

I reached up, anchored my other hand on something hard and metallic, curled my fingers round it to pull myself back up. I stretched my arm into the gap again. I could see the big concrete beam moving, slipping toward me. I stretched even more. I dug in my knees, gripped tighter with my other hand. Something sharp clamped round my wrist. Jack Pepper's teeth! I'd felt him do this before at the pond when he tried to pull me out. It hurt, but I didn't care.

"Hold on to me, Jack!" I shouted.

I pulled and pulled. I felt the hole give, his body move. I pulled and pulled until I felt him come free.

I hurled Jack into my chest, caught that dog in my arms just as the ground slipped away under us. I slid on my back, under the archway, to the ground. The fur coat protected us from scratches, but not from the thump when I hit the bottom. Above me the thin concrete beam tipped. The shadow blocked the light. It launched down the side of the pile toward us like a thick lightning bolt. I thought we were going to die.

I looked at Jack. The glisten in his eyes was alive. There was no fear, no tremble, no doubt that I would rescue him this time.

I realized what I was holding in my other hand

and suddenly I seemed to have all the time in the world. I whispered, "I've got you, Jack." I rolled, pulled Jack into my chest, and crouched over him. I put my arm over my head with what I still had in my other hand. Just as the concrete landed.

The smack of the concrete juddered through my arm; the pressure and weight pushed us to the ground. But what I had in my other hand was a Roman helmet, built to take the force of steel.

Jack blinked through the dust. I looked at the helmet. The thick crest on the top was bent and crushed. And we were still alive. I felt Jack's chest against mine, a faint movement from his ribs. He was so cold. He looked up. I saw Sirius, the eye of the Great Dog, brilliant even in the gloom of the massive sinkhole. Here, on Earth, with me.

"Were you still waiting for me, boy?"

I felt him wriggle, just a little, his tail swish softly against me. I was astounded by the life I could see in him, the heart of him, the brightness of him, even after everything he'd been through.

We weren't safe yet.

More broken buildings clattered into the hole. The ground rumbled and shook; dust showered us.

I put Jack inside my pajama shirt, tucked it into my pants. I did the fur coat up around us. I put the dented ancient helmet on as stones bounced around us. I scrambled, ran up the passageway, along the cells and walls and arches, until I saw the hole above me. I found cracks and crevices for my fingers and toes. I scaled that wall with Jack Pepper held tight into my chest. I felt the rush of air coming through the passageway, dust choked me, the crash and boom vibrated through me, until I hooked my hands over the edge of the hole in the wall in the dress-shop cellar.

I heaved us up, crawled in through the hole. Ran out of what was left of the building, over the wall at the back, along the alleyway, and crouched down behind the empty lot.

I pulled open the coat. Jack Pepper was gray with dust, his face sticking out of the top of my pajamas. So cold. I breathed and blew warm air inside my pajamas. I wiped away the dust around his eyes and mouth, his dry nose, brushed softly all over his face and ears, held him against me.

I swear that dog smiled.

Twenty-Eight

"Got you this time," I said. Jack's hips wriggled, his tail tapped against me, and I smiled. "You knew I would, didn't you?"

I wrapped that fur coat right around us again.

I walked through the middle of the silence on Clarendon Road.

I felt a stirring inside the coat. I checked on Jack, looking down into my pajamas when I could see him better under the orange beam of a streetlight. Jack wriggled. I felt his paws against me, his head push against the collar of the coat. His nose came out of the top, his head, just as the light dawned over Clarendon Road. Jack blinked; his nose quivered as he looked down the road.

The lion was heading toward us on the white line. His shadow grew as he passed the streetlight, stretched like a giant creature. He rippled and shook his head; his mane showered dust in a cloud around him, as if he was in a mist. He padded toward us and I kept going, and right at the last minute he jumped to the side and out of my way.

"Did you smell him, Jack?" I said. "Did you want to chase and play with him?"

I laughed up at the sky at Sirius, still burning brightly for millions of years. I turned back to laugh at the lion who got out of our way, at how he made our town his hunting ground, how Jack and me found a place in an amphitheater and won our fight. But there was no sign of the lion anywhere. Only Mrs. Pardoe's ginger cat disappearing around the corner.

Then I stopped. What was I going to do now? I had no idea what was going on at home, where I was supposed to be grounded. I was in so much trouble I probably wouldn't be allowed out of my room ever again. I didn't have a clue about how anything else was going to turn out except I had to take Jack Pepper home to Grizzly. It couldn't wait for another minute.

Grizzly needed Jack back so that the hole in his heart would be filled again by his daughter's little dog. And I needed to find a way to make it up to him for trashing his mobility scooter.

I took off the fur coat, wrapped it round Jack Pepper, and went into Grizzly's front yard. At Grizzly's door I laid Jack on the mat. Jack Pepper was the most loyal friend I could ever wish to have. He looked weak, thinner, but his tail wagged and his eyes glistened like stars.

I was sorry I'd ever told him to wait before, but I asked him now to wait again. "You stay right here," I said, and I knew he would. And I promised him with a thump to my chest that I'd wait, just around the other side of the wall, to make sure Grizzly found him.

Then I rapped that knocker hard, again and again, until I saw the hall light come on. Then I ran and hid behind Grizzly's wall, still holding the Roman helmet I'd found in the sinkhole.

"Dear boy, dear Jack!" I heard Grizzly breathe. "Dear, dear boy. What would Lucy . . . what would any of us have done without you?"

I knew just by the sound of his broken voice that all along he'd been so afraid for Lucy to lose him, not himself.

"Where have you been?" he said with nothing but joy at having that dog back. "Where have you been all this time? Causing trouble again, eh?"

It went quiet and I guessed Grizzly was holding on to that dog to make sure he really was here.

"What's this?" I heard Grizzly say. "What did you bring back with you, Jack?"

I was about to crawl away, to leave them to it, when Jack Pepper appeared round the corner of the wall, dusty and worn, but dragging the fur coat in his teeth. I didn't have any strength left for more lies.

Grizzly didn't come out to the pavement. He just said, "You tell that Leo Biggs he'd better come in."

I heard Grizzly's footsteps going back into his house. Jack kept standing on the coat, but he switched round and moved off it and kept coming, pulling as hard as he could. He dropped the coat at my feet as if it was mine. Then he stood there, all four unsteady legs square, looking at the coat and looking at me, and I looked at the fur, long and golden like a lion's.

Then Jack swayed and I scooped the lion's coat and that little white dog up in my arms and went into Grizzly's house.

Grizzly was on his knees when I went in, lighting his fire, Jack's bed still by the hearth where it had always been.

"Pass the coal bucket," he said, without looking up, "and a newspaper to fan the fire. We need to warm that poor dog's bones through."

We fed Jack, slowly at first, gave him plenty of water. Grizzly and I sat down and shared a pot of tea and ginger cookies. Grizzly snapped his in half and fed the pieces to Jack. We didn't stop looking at that little dog and Grizzly didn't stop repeating, "Dear, dear boy."

Grizzly poured some tea in his saucer and put it on the floor for Jack to drink and warm him inside. We made a hot-water bottle, we brushed Jack down; we wrapped him in a blanket and watched over him. This was no time for talk and explanations: it was time to take care of that little dog. We could see Jack didn't want to sleep, but he had to, his eyes slowly blinking, but watching both of us watching him. Then something seemed to satisfy him. He sighed, closed his eyes, and tucked his nose under the blanket.

Grizzly didn't look as haggard as he had when Jack had been missing, but there were deep, troubled lines in his forehead. He stood up, put his teacup on the mantelpiece, kept his back to me.

"Maybe Jack got trapped in a shed or garage," he said. "And couldn't get home even if he wanted to. Is that what happened, Leo?"

I swallowed. It hurt, like there was something stuck in my throat. Did he expect me to agree, to keep lying? Surely Grizzly guessed what had happened, where Jack had been, where I had been. But just beginning to tell the truth to the person you've hurt the most is the hardest thing. Knowing where to start.

"Jack was down the sinkhole . . . ," I began, but Grizzly had something else on his mind.

"You know I told you about that time I knocked out Nicky Sullivan?"

"I remember. All arms you were: he didn't see you coming."

"That's it," Grizzly laughed. "I knocked him out all right." He raised his elbows, curled his fists, punched out with his right arm, then jabbed with his left. His shoulders dropped.

"But it didn't count. Not there in the sparring ring on a Friday night at the club. Not without tickets and the bell and an audience."

That floored me for a minute, but I wasn't sure what he was telling me. Hadn't he been a boxer after all?

"I thought you said Nicky Sullivan said you'd make a good boxer. I thought somebody saw what you did."

"Oh, there was someone there. Sullivan's manager. And another person. They saw. Nicky's manager said I had a career in front of me. That I had a future in the ring. He could see my name in lights, you know what I mean? But that was before I knocked Nicky out. Nobody else ever knew, except one person."

Stunned, I realized Grizzly's finest moment had been hushed up for all these years. Except . . . Lucy knew.

"I didn't like the way Nicky spoke to the young lady who came in to clean the place. Sylvia." He smiled. "She became Mrs. Allen and Lucy's mom."

He recalled her, his face warm, his frown gone.

"No, no, I wasn't a boxer at Sullivan's club, not after that night. He threw me out and I joined another club; they were too embarrassed about what I'd done. The truth is I never won again. I had a few decent rounds and some success, but winning Sylvia's heart was the only real fight I won. Surprise you, eh?"

Well, yes, because he didn't seem like a loser at all. And no, because what I thought of him, even though it wasn't real, was much easier to believe.

"I think you're a champion," I said, because those big things about people don't change.

He growled a soft sound of satisfaction, deep in his throat.

"I won a prize more valuable than any shiny buckle around my waist. I liked that people thought I was a boxer and a good one at that, and I suppose I've let people think that all along. But the only fight I ever had was to win the woman of my dreams. And I'd rather you didn't tell anyone about that."

I opened my mouth. I guessed then that he did know what I'd done. Was he telling me that he wasn't going to say anything either? But I needed to tell the truth.

"Grizzly—"

"So what I'm saying, Leo, is this," he interrupted, his eyes casting over what I had in my hands. "The rest of the world doesn't always see or know what we've done. But we"—he pointed to his chest—"we live with it."

"And that's what made you great," I said.

He laughed, snorted, roared a big chesty laugh like a bear with a honeycomb, all the fear and dread and disappointment gone.

"It's what makes anyone great." He beamed like the sun rising and melting the frost on the window. "It's what makes that little dog great, what's inside him, what he's got in that little heart of his. And you only know it when you become like him."

All the time he'd been talking I'd had that Roman helmet turning in my hands, tarnished and dusty and buried for hundreds and hundreds of years below our town.

I thought of everything: of Warren and Grizzly's mobility scooter, of fame and praise, of Jack Pepper and the way he wouldn't let any of us down.

Then I told Grizzly everything that had happened, right from the beginning, and he listened and he didn't say anything but poured me tea and told me to keep going until it was all out, all finished and told, and became a story from the past to keep to ourselves and move on from.

"That Miller boy you talked about," he said, in the end. "Big lad, dark hair, shiny black bike?"

"That's him. Do you know him?"

"I met him a couple of weeks back coming home from town. I'd just gotten my mobility scooter." He sighed, disappointed in his own legs. "I was riding through the recreation field when I saw him. He'd fallen out with his dad." Grizzly frowned. "I think that kid has it tough at home, you know."

Suddenly there was a different Warren Miller that I didn't know. None of us knew.

"Do you think . . . he's pretending that he's tough then?"

"Maybe. Isn't that what we do when we're trying to defend ourselves? It's not the only act he has though. That boy is a lot like you in some ways." Grizzly smiled. "He dreams."

"He dreams?"

"He imagines he's someone else, just like you. Someone brave, someone who fights and wins, someone who others will be proud of. But he was embarrassed when I saw and asked him what he was dreaming of; ashamed that he pretends, that it isn't real. I told him it didn't matter, that it was good he knew who he wanted to be. But the boy was too upset. Perhaps I shouldn't have pried."

I understood then why Warren had done what he'd done to Grizzly and to me. You can feel really stupid when you think someone else knows what's in your imagination. He was trying to make sure he always had one over on me, just in case Grizzly had told me.

"What does he pretend to be?" I asked.

Grizzly's smile pressed into his cheeks. He didn't answer straightaway.

"You know what I was doing when I was going through the recreation field when I'd just bought the scooter?"

I shook my head.

"Pretending it was a motorbike! Chrome buffed and gleaming, the exhaust roaring like a lion!" He leaned back, recalled his scooter. "I don't think it would be right for me to tell you what that boy dreamed of though. That's up to him."

I nodded. I understood.

There was still a question left over though.

"Do you think it was Mrs. Pardoe's cat or Warren that kept knocking over your trash, Grizzly?"

"Is that what you're really asking?" Grizzly said, a twinkle in his eye. "Was Warren your downfall? Or did he show you who you didn't want to be? Do you think you can win without ever having to fight?"

They were good questions and I needed to clear my head before I decided what to do about Warren.

"Grizzly? I found something."

"So you did!" He roared, laughing like an erupting volcano. "So you did! I can see that; anybody could see that if they knew how to look."

I knew he was talking about something invisible inside me. But it wasn't what I meant.

"This," I said, holding out the helmet.

Grizzly was suddenly quiet. He took the helmet,

rubbed at it with his sleeve, saw the warmth of the metal under the dust.

"Put it on," I said, and he did. I could just see his eyes and the gladiator he was. "It fits you!"

Jack's nose came out and glistened by the crackling fire. Grizzly took off the helmet and beamed.

"If we're not going to tell anyone about getting Jack back . . . ," I said, and there was a question in Grizzly's face too. But I knew right then what I was going to do. "I still think everyone should see this."

Grizzly tried to hand the helmet back, but I'd finished with pretending to be a gladiator. I also wanted Grizzly to have a prize, for the fight he won, the fight nobody ever knew about. "I want you to have it. I don't want to be a gladiator anymore."

"No, of course not. Why would you want to be what you already are?"

"I don't want people to know what I did," I said, suddenly realizing that I wasn't going to get away with everything and that I could live with what I'd done all by myself, with just Grizzly and Jack knowing.

"Things like this can't stay hidden though." Grizzly

beamed as he cleaned the helmet with his sleeve. He nodded to himself. "If you're sure . . ."

"Totally," I said.

"Then leave your dad to me," Grizzly said. "Come on, let's get this all sorted out."

Twenty-Nine

A couple of days of good food and warmth and water and just about the whole town knocking on Grizzly's door to see the little dog from the sinkhole, gushing and fussing over him with bones and treats and biscuits, and Jack Pepper quickly recovered.

Reporters came; photographers came. Grizzly Allen, a great bear of a man, held that little white dog with the ginger mask in his arms and told them a story while they took pictures of them both standing in front of the museum with the find of the century—a bronze and gold Roman helmet.

It made the headlines of all the local papers.

Grizzly told everyone the story. It wasn't true, but it had all the things a good story should. A cat, a sinkhole, a meteor, and our hero, Jack Pepper. Grizzly told everyone that Jack Pepper must have fallen in the sinkhole, but was safe down the hole, and it took him some time to find his way out. When Grizzly found him barking outside his door in the early hours, Jack was carrying treasure in his teeth. He'd brought the helmet back with him. Grizzly could only assume that Mrs. Pardoe's cat had helped Jack to find his way out, maybe because Jack was so desperate to chase him, because the cat had been there in the middle of Clarendon Road too when Jack came home. Both of them covered in dust.

People loved the story. There were pictures of Grizzly and Jack, Mrs. Pardoe and her cat, the animals blurred in the photographs, wriggling and paddling, dying to chase each other still. Everyone loved Jack Pepper, not only because he survived the disaster, but also because he brought back something beautiful and valuable.

There was loads of interest in our town from charities, corporations, people who wanted to give money to build things, to start archaeological digs to find out if there was anything else underneath us, to expand the museum, to invite tourists. Plans and hope. To rename shops (Dad wanted to change his shop to Ben's Gladiator Café, but Mom told him not to). The buzz was immense. It affected everyone. The helmet was bronze with gold decoration, which meant it had belonged to somebody very important, so there was history beneath our feet and the possibility of more treasure to find.

I might have been wrong about the amphitheater though. I still don't know if I imagined it or not. Of course Grizzly couldn't say what I'd told him I saw down that sinkhole, and Jack couldn't have told Grizzly what was down there either, so Grizzly just had to leave things and hope people's imaginations would fill in the rest.

Most people were saying there was a Victorian sewage and cellar system under the intersection and maybe the helmet had been stolen or lost from somewhere else and hidden. People imagined all sorts of explanations as to how it had got down there. One day soon they're going to dig to find out the truth.

Grizzly told the same story to my family. He

told them the only reason that I was with him that morning was that I'd gone to his house to apologize for everything I'd done wrong.

Kirsty and Milly didn't say a word. As far as they knew, that's what I'd done as well.

I didn't hear the rest of the conversation with Grizzly, but Dad and Mom came up to my room. They stood there for a long time looking at me and each other. But I had some things I wanted to say.

"I'm sorry I let you down." Mom covered her mouth with her hand and shook her head. Dad put his arm around her. "It was all stupid and I'll never do anything like that again. It's just . . . well, I just kind of felt left out, and that I didn't ever do anything to make you proud."

"But we love you just the way you are," Mom said.

"Couldn't be prouder of my little daydreamer," Dad said, his chin trembling.

"We're sorry," Mom said. "We've always been proud. Perhaps we should have said."

"And you put things right, son," Dad said. "Can't ask for any more than that."

Then he opened his arms and it was all over.

"And you know what, son?"

"What, Dad?"

"What the special ingredient is?"

I stood back to see his grin.

"Pepper!" I said. "It's pepper, isn't it? Like Jack Pepper."

"No." He chuckled. "But that would have been funny." He smiled. "It's a good heart, the secret ingredient. Not the fancy type, just simple, plain old goodness. What I see in you, son."

Thirty

The last evening we had with Jack Pepper, Grizzly and I were sitting on his sofa when Lucy came back from her vacation.

Jack Pepper was Grizzly's daughter's dog and now she was ready to take Jack back home.

Imagine that.

Imagining is the only way you're going to know what it's like to have that dog turn up on your road, like some fallen star from the universe come to show you things great and miraculous, and then have him taken away again. And what you imagine will be nothing like how hard it really was to see Jack Pepper go.

Grizzly and I didn't move, each of us with a hand on Jack when Lucy came. Jack was pleased to see Lucy. His hips wriggled as his tail swayed, but he didn't know what to do. He jumped off the sofa, ran up to her, came back and jumped up, then down again.

Lucy looked at our battle-worn faces but saw our hearts were full. She smiled and shook her head.

"So what's Jack done this time?" She laughed and Grizzly told her his story too. "Always when my back's turned he goes and gets into all sorts of mischief. What will I do with that dog, hey, Dad?"

I don't want to say any more about what happened next except that, when they left, Lucy was baffled and amazed at the people from our town who lined the streets and cheered and waved as she drove off with Jack in her car, him looking through the window and leaving us with something more valuable than you can ever imagine. He was like something precious from a museum, something to keep for good inside us, something we could go back and look at time and time again.

So, Warren Miller. The thing was he wasn't so bad and I kind of understood him after Grizzly told me how he knew him.

I knocked on George's door.

"Well?" he said, all impatient.

"I'm sorry," I said. "I meant to say it before, but I couldn't—"

"Never mind that," George said. He grinned like nobody's business. "The map, Leo. The map!"

"Oh, that. . . ." I couldn't tell George now either! "Yeah, it was . . . useful, but obviously I didn't need it because Jack found his way out."

"Yeah, right," George said. He punched his fist and elbow down. "Look, you don't have to tell me, Leo, because I understand and all that, but just give me a sign. You got Jack back, didn't you? And I helped, didn't I? With the map?"

I grinned.

"George, all I'm saying is this: Will you help me with something else? I still want to be your best friend."

George grinned. "Always have been," he said.

"I can't tell you what I'm going to do though, George. Just trust me." I thumped my arm across my chest. "I promise it's a good thing, on my honor."

"Your honor as a gladiator or as Leo Biggs?"

"Leo Biggs," I said. "It's just me now."

We went back to school and George and I sat on the far right of the middle row at our desk, but the view looked different from there now.

Beatrix Jones came and sat next to George, so now there were three of us, and George said we had increased our friends by a hundred percent. Awesome. And I needed both of them to help.

At break time, Beatrix went to Warren's corner in the playing field and told him that Mr. Patterson wanted to see him in the classroom. George stayed in the corridor, hung around as lookout to make sure Josh and Warren's friends didn't follow him in.

I was waiting for Warren in the classroom.

"Oh, it's you," Warren said when the door closed behind him. "The hero." He smirked, but his lip quivered and his smile fell. He seemed different, kind of unprotected, without his friends surrounding him.

"I know about you," I said.

Warren's cheeks flushed. He swallowed. But I

didn't want to lie or play games.

"I know what it's like when you think your dad's not proud of you," I said.

He turned away, shook his head, picked up a book on the shelf, and put it back.

He half laughed, but it didn't sound real. "You don't know anything, Leo. You're a dreamer—"

"And I'm good at it," I said.

Warren glanced over. He took a deep breath and seemed to decide something.

"Look, the game's over—" he began, but my head was clear and I knew what I wanted to say.

"It isn't, because you haven't won yet." I took a step toward him. "Do your friends know? Do you tell them what you dream about? Do they help you?"

"I don't know what you're on about," Warren said.

"Grizzly didn't tell me or anyone else what you dream of being," I said.

Warren looked up at the ceiling, closed his eyes, and sighed. I saw it sink in, that everything he had done to protect himself had all been pointless.

"I don't know who you pretend to be, but I know it helped me to imagine who I wanted to be," I said, because most of all I wanted to tell him that there was something worthwhile about dreaming.

But Warren headed for the door, shaking his head, his back turned.

"I wish I'd told my dad the truth all along," I said. "He just forgot to tell me he was proud, that's all. It didn't mean he wasn't."

Warren turned the door handle; the door opened.

"You can go if you want," I called. "I'm just saying, if you want someone to help you win your fight, I'll do it."

The door closed. But Warren was still inside the classroom. He didn't turn around, but something was keeping him there.

"George and me are on Clarendon Road most evenings. You could come too if you want. Any time. We don't have to do gladiators. We could do what you want." Warren half looked over his shoulder. "And Jack Pepper's coming back to stay at Easter. Come then if you want. He's brilliant, that dog, honest he is. If it wasn't for him I wouldn't know what it was like to be brave for real."

Warren turned around to face me. He looked toward the window, his eyes far away, as if he saw something in his imagination that nobody else could see.

"You ever imagined you're a knight?" he said, smiling his lopsided smile, like he was letting me into the biggest secret ever.

"Not yet," I said.

I punched my arm across my chest. He saluted back.

And that was enough.

Acknowledgments

Thank you from the bottom of my heart to my husband for his support and patience, and for lending me his ears.

I have quite a few nephews and nieces; they are all wonderful, but some of the inspiration behind the Biggs family children came from three of them: Kelly, Jack, and Leo. My family, as always, are my rock.

I'd also like to thank Dave Wraight from Dorset Search and Rescue team for sharing his knowledge. My apologies if I have not done them the justice that their vital services provide, but it was always about the boy and the dog.

I continue to feel privileged to have such a special agent, Julia Churchill, and team at HarperCollins making my own dream come true, especially Sarah Shumway, who has championed the books all along, and Katie Bignell and the team, who have refined and taken care of all the rest.